I0451642

THE ANSWER

THE ANSWER

John Fraser

AESOP Modern Fiction
Oxford

AESOP Modern Fiction
An imprint of AESOP Publications
www.aesopbooks.com

First paperback edition published by AESOP Publications
Copyright (c) 2018 John Fraser

www.johnfraserfiction.com

A catalogue record of this book is
available from the British Library.

First edition 2018, revised 2020, 2025

ISBN: 978-1-910301-49-4

CONTENTS

1   The Colours of Air   7

2   Peace and War   101

3   Interlude   164

4   The Answer   198

1

THE COLOURS OF AIR

'Grandfathers! Forward! Bring them on! They let you choose a nationality, even a document. But – of course, you'll be investigated.'

'JEAN-LUC,' says Mélusine, 'He read the poster. He won't admit – go a bit back, we mostly come from somewhere else. He can't make sense of it.'

'Political bombs,' says Angelina, her friend. 'They make monuments. Most just rip out the fittings. The air bombs – those lay flat. That's business. Or no business – quite another thing.'

'The *Battle of Algiers* – how I remember that!' says Mélusine. 'Now, it's only criminals...'

'We're moving,' says her friend. 'Somewhere with animals.'

'Oh,' says Mélusine. 'I wish ... But not with Jean-Luc. India, perhaps, the monkeys ... lewd brutes.'

'It's so confusing,' says the friend. 'Once there were Americans – they were everywhere. Now – there's sultans, tsars, and all these caliphates. Is it history or geography, dear Mélusine?'

'Go where there's trees,' says Mélusine.

⋆

'Do something!' says Mélusine. 'Something new, Jean-Luc, in real life, so you're not a suspect.'

Jean-Luc tells his friend:

'I volunteered – there's a mistake. They can cancel memories, not add them. They clean your brain – a brainwash, seems like a dementia. What new memories would you like put in, if they discover how? Germinal, they'll be: like – planting irises, taking off the falcon's hood...

'There's my head, lying open on a salver ... the mouth, slack, afraid, arrogant. The eyes look painted on.

'Someone crouched over racing binoculars is staring at my brain. Her sweater says "Wild Girl".'

'The guy with the chisel says – "Old movies! Dozens, useless. If only we could install new wonders... We might put in the Qur'an, useful, in the event you're asked. Or a Ramayana. The colours keep you pepped."

'"I'm into *War and Peace*," the woman says. "I take slow trains, I need peace sounding in my ears. They couldn't see at night back then, so they fought their wars in light of day."

'"Here come the movies!" shouts the doctor guy. "*Chistka!* Out with them, a purge, wash out the mud!"

'"The cinema! Distant hooves: candlestick cactuses, long guns, no reloads, the bangs get added later, hate is easy, but love – the camera has to look separately into each set of eyes, so love's diluted, you must infer ... wow! – she lifts her silks, clean panties you can bet, he has no problem with his buttons, here come the fogs, day into night, Gabin's stone face, the clang of trams, the occupation, guys heaping into trucks and trains, politics, the baby dropped, easy to forget a little one, the letter is mislaid, subtitle you can't read, everyone so beautiful you can't tell who from witch – the old are crones or sages, villains wear tall boots, and there's the spooky song, don't pay the orchestra, you hear it but don't see – music stretches all along, those horns sound like trombones, the darkskins are in rehab, a chance to chant and dance, the fraudsters sneer, mistreat their secretaries and oh no, he's fondling her, the spy is shot, the boss is dropped, a satisfying splat, will the princess jump out the cake, her contract says ... freedom, puppets, other worlds..."

'The doctor says, "We got rid of all that, we left a space that you could fill with learning Tagalog, last words first lines," he spins along... "Any goddam thing you like, you must be desperate ... you're empty now..."'

'It's your Ismaili forebears,' says Mélusine. 'Riding white horses, firing flintlocks. Distant hooves, Jean-Luc! Cleaning your head – that's a good show. But – old movies! Black. White. Sometimes sepia. I do grey, instead. You're without evidence, Jean-Luc. You could be an extremist, no one now would have a clue.'

He can't respond. She says, 'I've been with you longer than with all the rest, Jean-Luc. It's time for you to pack the scenery... Saddle up. And go!'

The tug of rival caliphates – he can't experience it. It's vanished, for him, gone for ever. Those visionaries – scattered everywhere ... old Marx, called the last Fatimid – all gone now, old battles, refought, reactionary... There's still some architecture, Jean-Luc thinks, the brain is structured like it was back then, the eyes lined up, dimensions still the same. Those horses – horses of Andalou... It's obvious they're Spanish – it isn't possible they came from over there, the other shore – 'no, no, the Arab steed is quite a different beast. It has round eyes, a squarer jaw...' It's history. 'Mélusine', he thinks. 'She's normal, changeable, demanding ... best be up and go, even before she makes you...'

He says: 'The guys we should have voted for – they talk of love, fraternity – their closets bulge with armaments.'

'Quite so,' she says. 'I told you – get your ancestry cleared out.'

'Mélusine,' he says, 'now, I'm emptied out: of all those hours, hours in the dark, of other peoples' hours. There's not much left of me.'

'Well,' says Mélusine, 'if you'll suffer from not having me, there's nothing I can do.'

'Now, we're all luxuries,' says Jean-Luc. 'We people. Ornaments. When we were humans, long ago, and one of us had died – the goat would not be milked. The gun not loaded, the poachers not awaited. What are we for now, Mélusine? Trying our hands at anything, nothing, retiring on to chairs...'

'Billiard balls,' says Mélusine. 'They kiss. They do not penetrate. They are a set – if one goes missing, you must take one from another table. Or think "that pink's a green" – for ever. It's order, Jean-Luc.'

'I'm so empty,' Jean-Luc says. 'I am the highest point, the human azimuth – reached after a short and troubled history. There's nowhere else to go. No more world. We ate it. I'm the last.'

'I'm sure everything you say is true,' says Mélusine. 'But not for me.'

★

'I see you want some solitude,' Amanda, village mayor, tells Jean-Luc. 'If you will watch over someone, some old guy, alone – until the death – you'll have his house.'

'You mean, I inherit all his solitude?' Jean-Luc asks.

'Think what you please,' she says. 'To me – it is the law.'

The house is nearly sunk, into the turf, the timbers' roots. No ox could climb on to that unstable roof and graze – maybe an emboldened sheep... Inside, the air is thick. He sees the guy, yes – he's near some happening...

'Oh no,' says the old guy. 'You've come to put me down? With iron-shod sticks?'

'No, no,' says Jean-Luc. 'I'm possibly your friend... I love your tree outside, with sugary plums -they call them "*cuisses de nonnes*", nuns' thighs...'

'I'm not one from hereabouts,' the old guy says. 'And nor are you.'

He's wavering back and forth, like water in the tide. He's not going anywhere, the tide goes in and out, it's still the tide, always there – the moon's connected in some way, indifferent... the pull of water linking up to this old guy; he feels a force, perhaps, one not going anywhere, not his force, not him...

'Would some religion be of use?' Jean-Luc asks, quite at a loss. 'They bring it in when hope is gone...'

'A little late now, don't you think?' the old guy says. 'What can you offer? What's your take on me? On where I am?'

'I forgot,' says Jean-Luc. 'Forgot all that. No one believes now in those old movies – every story with a plot, a climax. I got rid of them. Actors pretending to be people. Death used to come in quick-quick time, with wisdom too...'

'The roof!' the old guy says. 'Stash me up there!'

'I can't help,' Jean-Luc says. 'They say I had Ismaili ancestors – they roamed, they had the hope, the vision – not like those guys now, down there it's all smashed up... Every new place starts desolate.'

'I know all that,' the old guy says. 'It's rooted in us all. I ask a different thing: no wisdom, no peace, no future. Leave me up there, overhead ... the green roof...'

'Of course,' says Jean-Luc, though he won't accept a corpse up there, above his head...

'They call me Ali,' says the guy. 'I'm not the Ali some of you are waiting for, returning. It'll do, till there's no one left to call me anything.'

'I don't know anything about you, Ali,' Jean-Luc says.

'There's no documents,' Ali says. 'So you Fatimids are really in the dark. That's why you seek the light, perhaps.'

'Perhaps,' says Jean-Luc, who hasn't understood.

'It's all a history mystery,' says the guy. 'Knowing about it doesn't solve a thing.'

'I'll live it through,' Jean-Luc says. 'Life. Everybody else's too, trotting along in parallel. And then it'll all be over.'

'That's how I see it too,' says the guy – you'd glimpse an ebb and flow in him, although ... the tide: it's centuries since it worked, it doesn't clean. It's just a drag.

'Mélusine,' Jean-Lus says, not knowing what else to say. 'She was quite changeable.' He laughs. 'Until she dropped me – that was definite.'

'It's elephants,' says the moribund guy, Ali. 'They show them in a line, each holds the tail of one in front. That's in the book: they'd be idiots to do it in the life. Facts – those too don't follow blind – they recognise grey shapes, and latch to them.'

'Ali,' Jean-Luc says, 'maybe you feel love? In the movies, only settlers feel it, not the primitives. Actors too, perhaps – like those Japanese, "pretending to be animals". Pretence – it's more convincing than the real, I'm sure.'

'Oh no,' says Ali. 'Love. What good would that do? Where would it be?'

'Listen, Ali,' says Jean-Luc. 'These mysteries I'd never heard of – now's your chance. Pass them on, even if they're mysteries without the key.'

'What good would that do?' asks Ali. 'Not to be negative. Just realistic.' He whispers...

Jean-Luc reluctantly stoops down, and Ali's breath, like a springtime swirl, plays with Jean-Luc, his face, his dangling locks...

'Let me tell you a story,' Ali says. 'Everyone expects something new, that someone will come, that you can start again, your big plan, get it right... A person, even...'

Then – he's still here, but he's gone. That's a paradox too. Religion – they say we lived by that; together with the digging, winnowing, and trade. After Ali's death, the arcana are still the same. Jean-Luc has never heard of them, so he's no wiser now. But – he was fortunate: he got to see his brain, have it whittled down, cut out the second- rate...

★

'We were scared of him,' Amanda says. 'We didn't know if Ali wanted good or bad for us, nor even where he came from. Maybe he didn't want to fight, and ran, or maybe no one fought at all...'

Jean-Luc doesn't want to put him on the roof. With Mélusine, he'd watched those movies – with Ali, there was nothing much to watch. No one anyway believes there is a someone waiting somewhere coming to punish everyone...

'... not scared of the person, obviously,' Amanda goes on. 'But of the context. Him – he went to death, you could say quite voluntarily – he wasn't sent. You watched – I'm sure you were compassionate.'

'The house,' says Jean-Luc. 'My due. It isn't much. A cold tap – needs connecting up.'

'That's it, then?' Amanda says. 'You're set for life, your past and future. Hmmm – you've not much cash. You won't go wild? Behave yourself, Jean-Luc, farewell and welcome!'

There's animals – they could be huge. Jean-Luc shoots out with the gun he's found. There's blood – blood on the leaves. Mélusine had told him – 'The animals – they're opportunist, humorous sometimes, routine and jealous.'

'If they come for me,' Jean-Luc said, 'I'll shoot at them. They sound like you, us all. There's nothing personal...'

'No! Jean-Luc,' said Mélusine. 'You shouldn't do that. Don't shoot! People will leave the food for you that they don't want ... make do! Don't hunt.'

'I wouldn't eat the carcasses,' Jean-Luc said. 'It's carrion that's lived on carrion. Besides, there's farms around with massacres of beasts – so delicate and trusting...'

'Nonsense!' said Mélusine. 'Fend for yourself!'

And that he does – it's dull. He notices – the stars have multiplied – heaven's abundant, but there's a mesh all over, it's like a cemetery at night, each faint starry bulb has invisible insects circling round, they're black, with carapaces, each one has tinier insects circling round, clinging on, some probably in red silk tights ... down here – the country – it's darker than in town, where there's a few, random holes above, as if someone had packed a cartridge, fired up, into the black...

*

'You're a suspicious subject,' says Amanda. 'You should find work, Jean-Luc. Trap beasts, trim trees. Run naked, howl at the moon – give us some clues...'

'When you've done everything, and stopped – you look back, and see a void. Just growing up.' Jean-Luc orates and weeps.

'Maybe you didn't do it right,' Amanda says. 'What you've done can't give satisfaction.'

'What will come next, then?' Jean-Luc asks. 'Will it be fascism? Will I be safe?'

'You're lucky,' says Amanda. 'You know what the words mean. Fascism. Safe. What else? Wild horses' sweat, Jean-Luc. How does that taste?'

'It's good, Amanda,' Jean-Luc says, 'but one craves variety.'

'Pfizz': on principle, he fires a soft shot, over her head as she departs. It falls gentle from the leaves – birdshot.

★

'Jean-Luc inspires.' says Mélusine: 'If he had had his brother – lost in the womb,' she tells her new friend, Sami. 'One could have been brilliant – the other, there to write it down.'

'Sex is my gift,' says Sami. 'Not inspiration.'

'I don't think it is a gift,' says Mélusine. 'Gifts are useful, or you can recycle. Yours is more a lobster dinner.'

'The great change came,' says Sami. 'When the white roads were tarred – people could scoot around on all that black.'

'What I want is – get away from countries,' says Mélusine. 'I had a salon, like de Staël. Being big poppies in Germany, or France ... you have to cook, stay sober; and it's small! Too many people on the run. Flux, souls sold in bundles, firewood. What does "meaning" mean, we asked. Not many answers...'

★

'We need your house, Jean-Luc,' Amanda says. 'You can't stay here...'

'It's my statement,' Jean-Luc says. 'Wild things howl by night, by day the flies clean up the mess. It's good. It works. You gave, Amanda – you can't take away. A word's a word.'

'Oh, but we may want to use the trees,' Amanda says. 'There's refugees and hermits, people throng the woods to rave... You can't have all this for yourself. All around, Jean-Luc, ever since you started coming here ... suspicious movements...'

'I had my say about all that. Sex, war, movies...' says Jean-Luc.

'We need your space,' Amanda says. 'Having your say's no guarantee of anything. No retreats into the wild, Jean-Luc.'

*

'Mélusine,' says Jean-Luc – 'I've been evicted. Just for a while, let me stay here, with you...'

Amanda thinks. 'Here, I want no killers, no sowers of dragons' teeth, no true believers. No enthusiasts, no visions – just the people running ... grateful, manageable ... let them come, and not complicate my life.'

*

I tell Jean-Luc, 'You should have refused to leave.'

He says, 'What do you know, cretin?'

I tell Sami, 'It's hard having to stay here with you and Mélusine, even without Jean-Luc...'

'Well,' he says. 'Why are you here?'

'I was awarded money,' I tell him. 'But they must have sent it to the wrong bank here.'

'That's really tough,' says Sami. 'The toughest thing. Could last for ever.'

Sami says he deals in semiotics. 'That's seeds,' he says. 'One seed looks like another. But the green part – they do that for themselves.' It's his little joke, of course.

Sami hopes sex is there just for itself – no sign, no signifier, no significance – like a sneeze. No after, no before, no web of anything, no culture and no name. In his experience no one thing leads on to another thing, nor is dressed in anything at all. It all comes in, to order: you lay things out.

'Tell me Sami,' I say. 'Who's the more brilliant – Mélusine or Jean-Luc? What they say – you can see it all on TV. Maybe it's them that's said it...'

'Don't be a smartass,' Sami says. 'However down you feel – culture must be produced, or else the whole ship stops.'

'Your ship sprang a leak,' says Mélusine, laughing. She and Jean-Luc think Sami was wrong to run away ... explosions, foreign soldiers... You must tough it out.

I tell Sami, 'I suffer for you Muslims, suffer terribly. My respect for the culture – I have a little flag – *Bismillahi rahmani rahim*... You recognise it?'

'To me, you don't seem like a Muslim,' says Sami, quite aggressive. 'If I told you I was an Iraqi Jew...'

'It's the same,' I say. 'I'm a scholar, I know all about that, the history.'

'We could have done with you,' Sami says, 'when the going was really tough.'

He calls to Mélusine, and they go in the bedroom, Mélusine really can't spare the time, she says. She's too thin for a good frolicking.

★

'What's this today?' asks Jean-Luc. 'Hotel Pirandello? Hotel Beccaria?'

The stairwell is a rhomboid, looking down, you think of Doktor Caligari, Nosferatu, you long to throw yourself spinning to the vestibule: – the glass dome is full of stranded frantic birds – the tear gas from the street accumulates...

'Amanda's in town today,' Jean-Luc says. 'I'll be there for her – there's a demo of the homeless...'

He's kitted up – a helmet and bandanas.

★

At the end – here he is, a parrot's egg over an eye; a rock or club?

'The cops are here,' says Mélusine. 'They know about you – your fathers were Assassins. Worse – they smoked hash... The coppers have you every way...'

'This too is culture,' Jean-Luc shouts. 'Me, the Neinsager. Celebrating what hasn't happened – fighting for the negative. A house. Who wants one? Better to stretch out on hot sand. Turtles, Mélusine – they bury eggs and weep, and when it's more than thirty-two degrees – all the hatch is female! Every one. The cool ones – are the males. A battle in the street – should make me valuable. I need stay cool...'

'You've an agenda, Jean-Luc,' Sami says. 'You want to shape occurrences. Just let it happen to you, like I did.'

'How'd I know what guys smoke, when they come here and freeload?' Jean-Luc shouts, glaring at me. 'They're all heretics – the Jews, the Muslims, the true believers – God, heretic supreme – those rules, jottings on a stone envelope, broken from the start ... unloving father – quite inconsistent, all family, favours, clients – sacrifices and piety, "oh no, no golden sculptures, please – that's too Jeff Koons – just your leaden souls abandoned like odd gloves outside my prissy paradise" – that's the request, a modest one...!'

There's a new postulant with Mélusine – a guy, Karlheinz. He calls his writing – 'The Illusion of Disorder'. 'We're all innocent,' he says...

'No, no, Karlheinz,' Jean-Luc shouts. 'You won't find me protesting for the innocents! Bomb them all – bomb the bastards, those innocent desires...

'Jean-Luc, go easy,' Sami says. 'It's awful taste! Apologetics for the terrorists...'

'This is the end, Sami, my unadorable friend,' Jean-Luc shouts. 'Down it all comes. Capitalism – it makes the war, and then it needs the peace to build up inventories... Bombard the houses, till there's no one left to buy Ferraris and vibrators – walk the streets in hunger and in penitence, wear binliners, defer to everyone, eat cats, no thought but prayer, infinite, unanswered – that's what you deserve – rise every morning to a plate of ash, work in the white-hot foundry every day and toss in panic on your bed of planks...'

'Well shouted, Jean-Luc.' Mélusine comes from the bedroom where she's entertained some cops. 'And all of you, especially Sami – no more your grotesque members in my delicate flower... Away with you –' and she turns to the police. 'Arrest these hooligans...'

And they take Jean-Luc away.

'His cobble only pinked a guy,' says Mélusine. 'His throwing arm's no use.'

'I see the opening of a little article,' Karlheinz says. 'His rant's right up my speciality...'

'Oh, he'll be let out in days,' says Sami. 'He's quite famous – he can't disappear.'

'Well,' says Mélusine. 'I don't want him here. You're right, Sami – a bad taste. That's what he's left.'

We hear Jean-Luc shouting in the street – 'I'll dynamite the shack. That'll deter Amanda!'

'Those cops,' says Mélusine. 'So encouraging, and so approachable. They come from stews and slums – each one. They grow up hitting, taking dope – but when they get promoted, into bourgeois clothes – there's a new start. What Gogol doesn't say. They show it's possible...'

'Mélusine,' I say, 'What if I had the treatment Jean-Luc had, and clean the marionettes and monsters from my head...?'

'You're much too young,' she laughs. 'The movies that you've seen have all been concocted, scarified – distant bombings, starvation at extremes... Hungry? Try to digest the grass – it all takes time and intimacy, my dear. Just cutting it all out – that is the easy way. I don't belittle it, of course...'

'It's good Jean-Luc is doing modern things...' I start to say. Protest. It sounds foolish.

'China!' says Mélusine. 'They must have modern things – to me, they do it all with hands and feet. They should invite me there.'

That sounds not quite foolish, but not wise.

She asks me, 'You find me reactionary? There's reaction going forward, and reaction going back, of course.'

'Well,' I say. 'You need a context. If you need a place to stay...'

'You have to live things through,' she says. 'It takes time. Lots of time is what you'll get, if you start murdering. Time all locked in. But then – it all depends, who and where. If you've a licence, shoot! It's heroism. Some animals are so noble, it's an honour to have them eat you up.'

'It all sounds philistine,' I say.

She's silent. I feel foolish. Maybe these people are quite wrong for me.

'You can't live here,' says Mélusine. 'Karlheinz is cleverer than you, and funnier. He has the better claim. In your case – you haven't needed to reject a teleology. That's the disturbing moment. How does it go on, after? Time, life, the progression – steamroller or butterfly?'

I hadn't realised – our chatting's an exam.

'A little lie, about your cash?' she asks.

'Mélusine, you're sweet,' I say – she hugs me, and steers me to the door.

★

On the stair, I see Karlheinz: 'If you want cash, my friend,' he says. 'Iraq, Syria – Yemen. I just came back. Black market! Immense.'

'You travelled, Karlheinz – that must make you a philosopher,' I say.

'Oh no,' he says. 'I'm in the electronic banking biz – there's opportunities...'

'Risky places,' I say.

'Everywhere is risky, those were very risky. You'd expect that when everybody's there from everywhere. Great guys,' he says.

'Maybe I'll ask you where my money goes,' I say, pushing past and down.

★

'Danger, Karlheinz,' says Mélusine. 'Tell me how it is.'

'When a shell bursts,' Karlheinz says, 'you hear nothing, there's no displacement at the first – then, the colours of the air – they leave you speechless – you're quite deaf, the air is grey, then orange, nacre...'

'That's about what I'd expect,' says Mélusine. 'I even read it somewhere...'

'It happens to be true,' says Karlheinz. Stiffly. 'Then – you are in danger. Maybe at that instant, you don't feel it...'

'No, Karlheinz,' says Mélusine, 'that isn't it. It looks like drama, something you dress up to do. But it's the system, Karlheinz – it can't survive, can't operate in its old way. So, how will it degrade? Is this the long, long ending inherent in its birth? A cracking of the edifice, without the crowbar you can use to make the whole collapse...?'

'You'd need to read my book,' says Karlheinz. 'It's all in there.'

'I think,' says Mélusine, 'if you can't tell me what it says, you didn't really write it.'

There's a silence – neither feels like breaking it.

Then – 'You must have left a mound of anger, Karlheinz,' says Mélusine. 'That's risk that you can calculate. Cinders from space, tumbling down, random – that's the same risk for everyone, incalculable. Sami's never angry. He's round, you can push him easy. Not love, not moderation: anger, Karlheinz. That's the potion – a poison that will swell you up, empower your fists and knock down giants.'

'And you, Mélusine?' Karlheinz asks. 'It is as good for you?'

'Oh yes,' she says. 'It's my escape – this "here" that isn't here or anywhere – I've been a shepherd of the docile tastes so long! Weep as you eat the lambs! It's not ideas and little articles, Karlheinz – walls aren't cast down by those – only the fury to destroy can change the landscape...'

'Yes, Mélusine,' Karlheinz says. 'It's not at all what I had thought. But – maybe you're right...'

'Oh don't for fuck's sake go away and change your manuscript,' shouts Mélusine. 'Act, if you can. If not – stand back.'

'I gave people what they asked: the price of course was what *I* asked,' Karlheinz says, retreating.

'No!' says Mélusine. 'Karlheinz – don't chicken out. You're not into therapy. Rehab? If you go there, don't prattle about love! It's order that you crave – everyone in quiet and modesty, scrabbling to fill the pot with oats and muddy water, off to the school so's they can write petitions, ask for loans they can't pay back... Anger, Karlheinz, not hypocrisy, that's you. Not making it like it was before it all fell down, the fire, the flood, the crazy priest...'

'This is Vito,' Jean-Luc enters, very positive. 'He makes the strongest hooch there is. It tastes the bitterest, but makes you drunk at once. It is a palliative, and that is what we need: escape that's going nowhere.'

Here's Vito, his red face has rarely seen the wind or sun, two little eyes as if the cheeks were stung by bees. 'Yes,' he says. 'Don't sleep if you've drunk this – you'll piss the bed. Dance till the dawn. If you can't stand, lie on the floor but twitch, or else they'll bury you.' He drags a wire cart, a big jar, large enough for pickling dwarves. 'They'd run out of demi-johns,' he says. 'This is a john.'

'I really shouldn't,' Sami says. 'What ignorance,' Jean-Luc shouts. 'The book – I don't remember which the sutra is – says ignorance is the excuse that losers use.'

Jean-Luc passes round the jars, Vito fills them from a ladle tall as himself.

'Now look, you guys,' Jean-Luc says, taking out a little telephone. 'That hut – where Ali died – I set a little bomb – it goes off when you telephone – but I forgot the final numbers...' and he grins round at the other drinkers... 'Each of us can try – we'll never know who was the lucky one... There's no one there, for sure...'

They all try, fumbling, giggling – Karlheinz dials up several times.

'Now, the TV,' Jean-Luc says.

Up comes someone, a glum face...

'Oh dear,' says Mélusine, refilling. 'Poor Amanda: the hootch, the thatch – they all caught fire, she, Ali's corpse... The still. What luck – you and Vito here, with witnesses.'

'I'll drink to that, dear Mélusine,' Jean-Luc says, and does.

'Sami! Sami! His moving finger did it, that's for sure,' they shout. '"City of Peace"! That's where he's from... He thought the world was his...oh the pretension, the hypocrisy...' They bundle him outside the door, Jean-Luc puts the telephone in his hand. There's no injustice done. No one is caught, no one is sought...As for a signifier... Sami can't remember anything.

'That's it,' says Jean-Luc. 'Retribution – is mine.'

'This stuff tastes of wormwood,' says Mélusine, pulling a face.

'Real wood, real worms,' says Vito.

'It's pitiful, Jean-Luc,' says Mélusine, quite sober, it seems. 'No boundaries redrawn. No cause betrayed or justified: no tit, no tat.'

'Dance with me, Mélusine,' says Karlheinz. 'I don't want to piss my bed – and I must speak tomorrow.' And so – they dance till dawn. 'Banks and power,' says Karlheinz. 'People have power, and so do banks. The people – have power when there's a majority; minorities? Too bad. The power's to make representatives who have the power. But moral authority, justice, and truth, no people can have that –

religion used to make the claim, though now, science claims the truth. Who claims justice? Well, people's power's a slippery thing. Then – banks: they're not science, not religion, nor philosophy – you need a place to stash your cash, but you could improvise... So, what they have's the power to take your cash, and lend your neighbour's cash to someone else – yours too...'

The wormwood's bitter in his throat. Where does it lead, the rant?

Jean-Luc asks, 'Karlheinz – what next? Faith? Submission?'

'I don't know,' says Karlheinz, 'I expect it's all of that.'

*

Mélusine says, 'Jean-Luc's details have come back. He's not a cosmic missionary – it isn't in his blood. French cows. Those are all that's in his ancestry...'

'Oh,' says Jean-Luc. 'You can't trust that. Not history. Our species – we shan't be here much longer, – it's happening all too fast, too violently – galaxies and gas and gods, all tumbled in.

'And – by the way, Karlheinz – the cash you made, where did you bank?'

'Bank?' Karlheinz says. 'What money? You can't trust rumours, Jean-Luc. Honest cow-herds, your family? Maybe prisoners from Roncevalles?'

'I miss the cows,' says Jean-Luc sadly. 'Look how bourgeois we all are – is this the way it all must end? Vito, our only proletarian – and now he's lost his still, his one fixed point...'

'It's not a comeback,' says Mélusine. 'The bourgeoisie – it never went away. They look up through telescopes, take your money, do philosophy, send you off to shoot your brothers. They're aristos – there's no pop scene left for everybody else – so, what's left? Prayer?'

'You can't have social classes and democracy,' Karlheinz says. 'There's ways to end the world, Jean-Luc, but setting bombs is infantile...'

'Let's get this straight,' Jean-Luc says. 'We didn't set a bomb. The telephone – was just a game, to see how far you'd go. Natural causes. Poor Vito's livelihood.'

'Innocence reborn,' says Mélusine.

★

There's a mousy sound outside the door.

'What's that?' shouts Mélusine, sensing interruption, 'Sami's cut flowers? Apologies and peace? Mutilated greenery? Death? – just like him, these guys with paradises in their culture – quite intolerable for other people, justifying everything...'

'It's me, Solène,' says a waif, shut out. 'Amanda's daughter. She said to come to you, you believe in helping people...'

'Yes, true – that's our belief,' says Mélusine: 'There's lots of idle guys, reactionaries all – who use their sarcasm on that count. Our belief's important, it's action for us – we can't all bind up wounds, carry white flags ... make martyrs' videos...'

'Yes, yes,' says the mouse Solène. 'I don't seek board, dear Mélusine, just a bed.'

'We did that at school,' says Mélusine. 'The mouse says that to Asclepiades, the Greek miser. I'm not a miser, dear Solène, though my school prepared us to be rich. Don't quote at me, dear – I'll win!'

'Only a bed,' Solène says. 'No education, please.'

'We're in a crisis here,' says Mélusine, using both arms to keep the strong mousy girl immobile by the door. 'The world, the ferment... How far do we let it go, does universal war conclude in universal peace? Jean-Luc's on one side, I'm unclear... at any rate, I don't use public transport, don't make myself a silhouette. You can't trust anyone.'

'Of course I understand: my mother,' says Soléne, pushing Mélusine aside. 'Vaporised. A cause surely not her own... History, the juggernaut...'

'Then,' Mélusine goes on. 'There's the offer of emotional satisfactions I don't want. The disturbances! Some randy guy... They stick to you in courting. Trying new foods, and poetry. Really, one wasn't born for that... Vaporised, you say? The funeral send-off – it could be a delight, if sensitively done... The dove ascending as pure thought ... no ash, just air...'

'White air, with just a scroll of red,' says Solène. 'That was what they said.'

'Oh well,' says Mélusine. 'Life or death, taste doesn't enter... Then, my dear, there's all the sex, corked up in retorts that I don't want...'

'My mother, and Jean-Luc – a classic tale. Remember the snake that did for Eurydice – something of the sort did for their love,' says Solène.

'To save your time, my dear,' says Mélusine. 'Don't imagine I was that asp. Nor that Jean-Luc admits to anything at all.'

'I see,' says Solène. 'There's just the one room for all of us. I can make do.'

'Are you sure?' asks Mélusine. 'It's not the country here. You say you love your animals before you slaughter them – here, we don't love, though slaughter – that's a current talking-point. Ask Jean-Luc about it.'

'Oh, but we don't farm,' Solène says. 'With us, it's finding guys who'll fix the thatch and bottle herbs. Grow pot.'

'Everything here is delicate,' says Mélusine, closing out. 'You country types, you keep things clean – it's being around sick dirty animals – maybe you would sweep a bit, go to the market, all that stuff...'

*

'Jean-Luc!' says Mélusine, overloaded, when Solène's been cemented in the ménage. 'Amanda's daughter, Solène's here. You're in the middle of your plot. Your daughter, maybe – and you vaporised her mother – Solène seems docile. Maybe you're not related – that's an advantage – but then there's Ali, your house, the bomb...'

'Oh no,' says Jean-Luc. 'There's no mystery. Let her doss down, and revel in the to and fro. Frolic in the revels! Above all, my benevolence – like warm wings...'

'I have a difficulty too, Jean-Luc,' says Mélusine. 'Too many friends. There's Karlheinz, Sami – maybe you. The pricking of desire I had for Vito: even that youth we sent away, much duller than Karlheinz, but maybe less obnoxious – all offering a courtship unsolicited... I'm like the crab that once a century may come on heat, and leave a twist of yolk under a frond, and many many years go by – perhaps some ancient crusty type, a lobster fogey – will smell the smell ... and slowly, slowly from his shell...'

'Yes, yes, dear Mélusine. Your problem is the same as states'. Follow your interest, you aspire to have a major enemy and many friends. But – it happens, that when you follow logic, your interests – you end up not with one great enemy and many friends – but many enemies. No friends.'

'Well, that's too bad,' says Mélusine. 'You hold your nose, and sort it out.'

'It isn't so,' Jean-Luc says. 'Not now. Fights to the death. No longer champions and chivalry – but cultures irreconcilable, a great confusion, continental quadrilles, a brisk tectonic waltz... Once, the world was large, and each could have an empire as compensation for all other pains, now, that's not on...'

'Think of Solène,' says Mélusine. 'Her place. The plot is complex, but yours is the devious mind...'

*

You hear the shouting and the laughter, tears and whispers, from below. I climb the stairs.

'How are you, Mélusine?' I ask.

'Go away,' she says. 'We're in complexity.'

'Take a break,' I say. 'Months. That's what they say.'

'No,' says Mélusine. 'What did you want? Ideas? Your cash?'

'At present,' I say. 'I drive. Limousines. No tips – you have to behave like royalty.'

'We'll, you can stretch out in limos,' says Mélusine. 'The housing problem's solved!'

'I'd rather hoped...' I say.

'Well, there's Solène arrived,' says Mélusine. 'Full up! We have to sort where she fits in.'

★

Ah, Solène... Oh! Solène!

Her domestic's smock, undone ... how white she is, the ready fruit. 'Don't stare,' she says.

'I know,' I say. 'Exactly what goes on. Your context, Solène. These Southern towns, seething in grey dusty afternoons, solitude en famille, hot screwing on those wormy beds, sweat sticks, heads ache, recriminations – then, in the cool, the boulevards that run like termite mounds, and after, sleepless you toss and dream of fathers, moustaches pencilled in, Beretta in the drawer, and on and on...'

She asks, 'You. Do you have an offer? You know you can't come in.'

'I know about your mother: Ali, Vito, too. Him – Jean-Luc,' I say.

'I'm just a village girl,' she says. 'I don't do mysteries. Beg, that you want to take me with you – I'll say no, and jump into your eyes and stay for ever.'

Oh Solène!
None of this, of course.

★

'You can't come in,' Mélusine says to me. 'Already there's a plethora of characters and stuff we haven't thought about. Russia, for instance – that cold air in cubes that we could do with here – and Sami, weeping in the toilet... Why don't you...' and she pushes me against the door, my! a breathy gust – the mortadella she eats, garlic-powered. It's so hot, hermetic, under the beige glass roof... 'Go to the spot. It's true, we're mostly Arabs here, Turks and Iranians, others that they've never heard of here – go to their homelands. Go where there's danger, where you shouldn't go, you, passing for mestizo, renegade, blackslider, heretic – and fill us in.'

'Will there be cash...?' I start to ask.

'We'll send it to a bank, and have it wait...' she says.

'Solène?' I ask, despairing.

'Solène stays here,' say Mélusine. 'Amanda was political, and so what Solène does is suspect too. We'll have them clear the folklore from her head, the family and stuff, and she can start off clean. And cleaning's what she'll do, the dirt here multiplies...'

★

At the station, everybody is camped down. There's Arabs, Turks, true Turks, and even-truer Turks. The trains, the call to prayer – come from all over, El Cairo too.

I find a Kosovaran document, try it at a bank.

'Go away,' says the guy, the guard – just like Mélusine. I don't tell him I'm a scholar.

Propped against a wall – there's an old distinguished guy, nothing to occupy him...

'The marble floor,' I say. 'This is real class. There's muzak too – the pope says there's no purgatory. This isn't heaven, let's think it isn't hell...'

'Oh, you're right,' the guy says. 'I think the pope is wrong. These awful tunes...'

'Theology,' I say. 'Armed struggle, geopolitics – maybe you've some thoughts?'

'Oh,' says the guy. 'We talk about these all the time.'

There is no more to say. Maybe ... I should invent, and then interpret, like all scholars do. If only there was Solène here...

*

Oh no! Here comes Jean-Luc. 'Aha!' he says. 'You have the look of someone thinking how to cheat their boss! I'm the expert – but of course, I never made a bomb that caused the accident... How could I know?'

'We all know how.' I say. 'Look! A continent – no, half a globe – is lying on thin mats, there in the central station. Nothing exotic's left – no camel trains, no Syrian glass, no saintly monuments up like terra cotta thumbs, hitching to heaven, no princess lying in the permafrost... All fled away...'

'Yes, yes,' says Jean-Luc. 'We all know all that. Mélusine wants to be rid of you, gives you a task. There's nothing to be done. They'll fight it out for generations, everywhere, maybe we'll all die, each against all, who's bigger than the big, oh, the inhumanity, my dear – and in the end, no second comings, nor the first. Monkeys, my dear, each wired to the next, all knowledge on our little screen as we trudge into battle, our ape-long arms can scratch for mines as on we go, not breaking step ... those monkey corpses fit together, like a stack of plastic chairs ... there's no advantage in the splashy deaths of ones and twos – you need a hecatomb before it counts...'

'Well, Jean-Luc, what is your scheme?' I ask.

'Those guys who keep a million soldiers under arms ... or just a dozen, hungry in ratholes – hoping their death will help to bring a state with tickertapes and postage stamps ... that is the mystery. How's it done?'

'You want to be a general?' I ask.

'No, no,' he says. 'It's automatic, what they do. It's knowing *how* it's done. That is the trick, that once you know, the possibilities are great.'

We step among the Uighurs, Nepalese – 'You see,' Jean-Luc says, pushing me on a local train with plywood doors. 'These guys may lag in electronics, but they're wise. They're mostly driven from their homes by those they call their own... A new United State, my boy, is what we need, and what we'll get. Where to locate it? Where there are trees... I know – your mouth flaps open to object – 'beliefs'. Of course we must all believe the same – you can't have cops and soldiers forming fives and thinking, 'Well, hohum, maybe here and there the other side is right.' No, it's unanimity, or keeping quiet... The Russian said it well: 'Before everything – service'. Remember: *sluzhba*. Have you forgot already?'

'I've a passion for Solène,' I say. 'Her servitude – freeing the slaves is in our quest. Freed, then enslaved to the liberator – white as a root she is...'

'Yes,' says Jean-Luc, unsettled. 'Ginseng. You get it in the bars. Try unspooling what's in your head. I did: what you call culture – it can all be sluiced away. You feel lighter after, and it doesn't hurt at all.'

Outside, nature unscrolls. 'Cows,' says Jean-Luc, dreamily: there they are, black and white with jigsaw patches stencilled on: brown, scuffed like old Gladstone bags: devil-black, alone in a field, their molester's testicles heavy and threatening as brass cannon balls; pigs in zinc shacks, scrubbed cherry-pink, prime for the bacon slicer ... a creaking flight of swans, the turkey delicate, its psoriasis unscratchable, 'You must use your fantasy,' Jean-Luc says, 'or it's all unbearable. Ignorance: is their bliss, not yours. Think of your ruddy face, your grumbling belly, as you enjoy them, broiled and flayed...'

I try.

'Forget memento mori,' Jean-Luc shouts. 'Remember – you were born! You're on the slope, with all the rest, all in the danger, rolling down...Others will be born as well – better, much much brighter than you are, even than Karlheinz. Forget Solène – you'd drag her down, you evil bastard –' and he opens the train door, tries to force me out – he can't; the scroll you're on, it's not fly paper; you don't stick, the one dimension – you can't be erased so easily ...

'Here we are,' says Jean-Luc. 'Amanda's place.'

We jump down. 'As for Solène,' Jean-Luc says. 'I'll do a deal. Be realistic: that unbuttoned body – that will feed you fantasy – for all your life.'

'Oh yes,' I say.

'We know how love with sex works out,' he says. 'You've had your look. A kiss – the first and last. The meetings, looking into eyes – what do you see? You'll work it out. No touching. Lots of yearning – and a walk around the park. The cinema, the ballet, the picture gallery, all just once – no judgements and no arguments – just start up a clangour in your hearts, lay out the memories. Then stop! The partnership's complete. No further! No boredom, no fishing for the delicacies, no trawling for monsters, and no porn... Enough! A classic, it's all there.'

'It sounds a painful trek,' I say.

'Exactly!' Jean-Luc says. 'It's a collection, in your head, a living sliver from the past – a celadon, commode with ormolu, chryselephantine head – the nymphet's glance, the spell that lasts for ever – immaterial, immortal, the melancholic glimpse... The promise of the god, the goddess: 'I shall return, be yours for ever...' The prophecy? Hah! Silence. Absence. I promise, it's the best that you can have...'

'An empty life, Jean-Luc,' I say.

'And yet, the best, the purest, noblest anyone can have: fantasise, turn love into self-love, desire to useful energy. Be gay, hermaphrodite, whatever you could wish... She is inside you. You won't need cash, no prospects, no career, no trouble with your kids... you're safe. So's she.'

'Nothing, Jean-Luc,' I say, and weep.

'You're free!' he says. 'That United State, its citizens we saw, reclining on the marble floor, watching the trains that leave for everywhere, that they will never board – where shall we set it up? That is your quest. You'll help me find the spot...'

'The ethereal Solène?' I ask.

'I can fix it with her,' Jean-Luc says. 'She loves being taken out.'

On the village square, there's groups with masks and sticks, swiping at each others' heads.

'My philosophy, acted out.' Jean-Luc says. 'Amanda was to be my missionary. She backslid. I wrote this tome – even to cut the pages was a pain... It brought to mind the Japanese, their way with cutting edges. My book – 'The illusion of choice' – may die unread. It's not uncut. These martial arts I introduced – they think it's for the armed gangs in the woods. It cannot be – against those bullets you'd need amulets. It's not a force you want: it's disciplines. Lots of them. Sticks and sharp edges too. There's taking pain; pretending to be cowardly,' and he laughs. 'Oh, and strategy and geopolitics and rumination. You might say – the gamut.'

'They look quite happy,' I tell Jean-Luc. 'No backsliders. With sticks and swords – the villagers go to.'

He laughs: 'Oh yes, there's bets with phoney coins and saké too. There's something to suit everyone...' He pinches my arm, where it most hurts.

'You see,' he says. 'They have the fear that guys will up and run to join the religious nazi crew. When there's suspects, I'm afraid – they burn their house. It's so they won't come back. It isn't just, dear friend, but comprehensible.'

I see a painted sign. 'How to live a full life when non-being is the condition of existence.'

'That's the philosophy?' I ask Jean-Luc: 'Is my airy fling with Solène part of it?'

'Exactly so,' Jean-Luc says. 'Of course, Mélusine does not agree. She wants to catch the play of forces so she can step right in and change their flow. Contacts with the powers that are. Me – I look for space. We need to find an emptiness where all the people on their quest – call them escapees – can settle in and then start off again. It's a non-being that finds a place to live...'

'Like breathing in and out – the air, always invisible, and when you stop, there's none, and you are not,' I say.

'That's sort of it,' Jean-Luc says. 'But you should read the book.' He picks a stick and wham! upon the shoulders of some guy whose back is turned.

'You can be everything,' I say, 'in nonbeingness... Or nothing, even...'

'Fuck you!' says Jean-Luc. 'Any complex thought sounds idiotic if you want to make it so. Idiocy – that can be the highest tide reached by a philosopher – or the lowest ebb of idiots. In your case...'

★

Vito's turned from hooch to nature: here's his stall – the Jampot. 'The best smoke, sugared up, in jars: you spread it on your toast,' he says.

He has a sidekick now, Sylvain, a giggler. Toady.

'We are ambassadors,' says Vito. 'Watching Ali die – we thought a rustic way of cutting short the tears was on the cards. We cut – the highest card takes the iron bar – salutes the moribund, and – there's the end to it. The suffering: so, it's done, enough. There's gratitude. A fee. In the end, my friend, we're speechless animals. Like on the farm, we're reared to die: – but no one eats us. We're no use. Has anybody, in the moment of their death, had revelations? An epiphany? Naturally not. We're in line with Jean-Luc here...'

He gives his spiel, and Sylvain nods, and nods. 'The life beneath the everyday,' says Vito. 'That's what we reach to, and our mastery of self turns our gaze to beginnings, and their ends...'

'Tell me the whole tale,' I say, impatient, 'about Amanda. It's so harsh here, since she went...'

'I'll leave you,' Jean-Luc interrupts. 'Do your breathing, friend,' he tells me. 'And stick-work. Burnish your blade...' And pouf! he's gone...

*

'You dumped him, then,' says Mélusine.

'He doesn't know how hard they train now in the countryside,' says Jean-Luc. 'There are militias everywhere. It's tough. He'll need to find my book. I gave him the first discipline: the song says. 'I don't wanna feel blue any more...' and so – 'Sometimes – you have to forget about it.' That's to toughen him: he can't just wander, picking people up and feeling passionate.'

'Sami had his brain cleaned,' says Mélusine. 'Out it all came. The river, the weeping, the palms – upturned and empty. Those fat white cars, thin donkeys – out they went. Still he weeps. He's right in that... Karlheinz is here: he does his economics. It doesn't give us hope.'

'There's much paranoia around,' Jean-Luc says. 'Sami's an escapee, fear is their overcoat: suppose he and Karlheinz are into showbiz, big hollow money, or – they dig into parts of the computer that don't exist? They're perilous, Mélusine. Are you giving them the rush? Not screwing one at least of them? We've already had a death: Amanda – rocked the village. And you've no idea how many disciplines there are, and all the equipment you need for all those martial arts. Someone's laying into you with bamboo rods, a sharpened disc – which discipline is that?'

'Amanda was a politician,' says Mélusine. 'That's why this scamper started up. Of course, I deal with states – all shapes, all colours. Shake the kaleidoscope...'

'Yes,' says Jean-Luc. 'And all the colours fly, like dropping an aquarium ... places you never heard of, boil, the magma flows...Vito, now – he and his friend, they're hospice nurses. Extinction is their game. He's our go-between with nature. You must be good with maths: to save a species, bugs or bears – you sell another lot as trophies, use the cash for conservation. Is it wrong? They've no idea, the bugs. The bears – look how happy! Waving! It's worth the sacrifice... Sacrifice – they've no idea... Vito'll do what it takes, just ask, and pay the fee.'

'Sami now,' says Mélusine. 'He looks quite sick. His quest – maybe it's better ended now. You need a lab and funds just not to find anything. Imagine crying solo by the stream, the waste of spirit...'

'There!' says Jean-Luc. 'It's where we have arrived. It's not a river, Mélusine – it's a mountain. Those elephants – if one lets go the tail of one in front – do they all fall off the path and down the mountainside? We must join up... Everything.'

'They scream, those elephants,' says Mélusine. 'And you do too. Yet in you jump – an island for your escapees? Whose ocean do you put it in? Whose desert gets our water so your guys can get a drink?'

'Oh,' says Jean-Luc, 'my book shows how complex stuff that's not quite there holds us afloat, it teaches you the technique that you need to walk on air... Like a loan so big – can never be repaid, never on the books.'

'You need air that's solid as dynamite,' says Mélusine. 'Sleeping careful in its box. And then it isn't anything at all, it's blown, and everything has fallen down. It's like your debt – so huge – but you're feeling good, then there's a blip – you're lying broken naked, with no legs, and all there is, is dust,' says Mélusine.

There's silence, immobility. Jean-Luc looks round the dirty rooms. Then –

'Sort this place,' shouts Jean-Luc. 'Get Solène on her broom, throw out these gamma males! My book? Difficult, you say, Mélusine?'

'I never even saw it, Jean-Luc,' says Mélusine. 'Besides, you're too confused.'

'The trouble is, Mélusine,' says Jean-Luc, cooling off. 'Is we both want ways in. Inside, we want ways out.'

'Everyone says they want to quit,' says Mélusine. 'Because they don't know any ways at all: not in, not out. It's ignorance. They don't remember names – just faces. The powerful people – they don't have a face. Their hat falls directly on their shoulders.'

'Your trouble, Mélusine, is you're gullible,' Jean-Luc says. 'You think you deal with salted guys that steer those ships of state, who're qualified as matelots, that climb the masts like bonobos – but it's not so. The money, Mélusine! They've few years to take the cash that buys them refuge, and a stash.'

'What we need,' says Mélusine. 'Is a guide... A Virgil, cultured guy, who being spent, if not quite dead, arranges transport, identifies the landmarks, names the cadavers hanging quartered in their chains...'

'Well,' says Jean-Luc. 'If you can't use Karlheinz – there's Sami. He's ideal. Scene-shifter at the opera of Baghdad – he'll supply the backdrops and the curtains for all scenes that we could want. A shout alerts him ... and there is Florence, Damascus, the notary's snug, the poets' fug, the infinite storm, the desert where those princesses dry out in their oranges...'

'Yes, yes,' says Mélusine, excited, sceptical... 'So, our scene will change, the still point's us! We shall avoid the dangers of the train, the donkey cart. Of course, we'll need a majordomo, someone to tote our bags and tint our hair ... but there's Solène...'

'It's true,' says Jean-Luc, 'I did the test of loyalty. I came out clean, of course. But ... Fatima. She's somehow in my story, not my genes. The mystery of faiths, the bridge that joins them all ... and then the global plot, inspiring all those movies that I thought I'd lost... Of course, it's not my ancestors, the Fatimids, that make me what I am – it's my belief.'

'But, Jean-Luc,' says Mélusine. 'Fatima, the Prophet's daughter, the mysteries that obsess the popes – you don't believe in that – a gallimaufry, a printer's pie... That's not your ancestry...'

'Oh, Mélusine – that's a cover,' Jean-Luc says. 'If you have no vision – it's all wandering. You're lost. We need a code – it's obligatory for everyone who strides out on the earth.'

He says to Sami, 'You'll do that for us? Change the scene without we have to move? I bet when you had work, the opera played Le Calife de Bagdad,' he jokes, pinching Sami's arm where it most hurts.

'You're not the first to make that quip,' says Sami, backing off. 'And don't bring up Nabucodonosor. Verdi, Italy – all a big mistake...'

★

'Sweep, sweep, 'weep, 'weep,' says Mélusine, laughing as she shows Solène a heap of dust. 'It's being so high up – it brings the dirt, the flies... But you'll be with us, everywhere.'

Solène gives off a meaty smell, like catfood on the turn – Mélusine can't keep a cat, she's just a tenant, but, she says, cleanliness is next to heaven, she's up there, observing everything, whole cities, the motors flitting red and black.

Sami says, 'They say you want an Ismaili caliphate, Jean-Luc – you having ancestors...'

'Oh no!' says Jean-Luc. 'We ascertained all that. True, I've many things they had. The vision? Maybe. My expectations? That's for sure. The global view? That too. But,' he goes shyly on, 'my plan's for all the escapees. There's millions of all kinds who need escape. What I want's – a good America. No massacres, no guns. The guys would have no cash, no arms. If they need defend themselves, they'll need to have a proxy. Let's not dwell on that. Rich people do their business clean, with bombs and schools. Intelligence. Poor people – they cut off your tongue, and worse. We need an empty place, no one to call Indians; no slaves. The question is – where is this hidden continent? Not too big, nor small, nor too hot, nor cold – just right. Where there's sufficiency, so no one envies them. Not so barren they must sell themselves.'

'Well,' Sami says. 'Find it! I've walked and run – I never found the place. If you're successful, dear Jean-Luc, be sure I'd stand in line for my new documents, and have my brain cleaned, if it's necessary... Are you convinced, though, that there's such a place? Hidden but imminent?'

'No, Sami,' Jean-Luc says. 'If I knew, I wouldn't look.'

'It comes to mind, Jean-Luc,' says Sami, tears starting up again. 'How you once wrote about a similar scheme – resettlement, but where the guys you wanted to be rid of didn't want to go. Your moving finger wrote...'

'Oh scribble scribble,' Jean-Luc says, much irritated. 'One says these things, and then moves on.'

'If once it didn't work, maybe another time ... the same result.' says Sami.

'Well, yes and no, and maybe, too,' says Jean-Luc, quite exasperated. 'All you need do is shift the scene, Sami, put out a different flag, new decals on the lectern, flowers, all that, new principals. We'll do the rest. Cut deals with every cheese, big, small, and wormy... The guys, the escapees can wait: waiting is their speciality. The idea's good, we'll see...'

'If they won't go?' asks Sami.

'They've nowhere else. I sent out a guy – he knows what he should report. No homes, no water and no cash. Houses destroyed, militias, occupation, minefields everywhere. They'll want my solution, Sami. Karlheinz will find the cash – that is the easy part. No one wants them close...competing, doing everything better, singing at night...'

And there the matter rests.

*

Mélusine is able. There's conferences with all the great. Sami's a genius, arranging flowers and chairs, lecterns and fireplaces with no pokers...

'A fine idea, Jean-Luc,' says everyone, 'but not for now.'

'It's impossible,' Jean-Luc tells Mélusine, 'that there's no spare room for anyone, or if there is, it's uninhabitable. Karlheinz though – got promises of cash... What next?'

'Don't be demoralised, Jean-Luc,' says Mélusine. 'No one gives a territory away. The world's full up, there are no empty lands. Maybe escapees should go back – scrabble and die ... not rob someone else.'

'Those big guys,' Jean-Luc says, 'whose names I don't remember – we should have gifted gold to them, in sacks...'

★

'Act one of my libretto,' Sami says. 'The daughter mute, the mother dead. The principals are close – they split – then cling again, frustrated. The tension for the acts to come is in the daughter and the suitor with no name, obsessed and crazed, maybe the composer even...'

'No, Sami,' Jean-Luc says. 'The plot is mine, not yours. I spit on your conventions.'

'We're only at the start,' says Sami. 'It all works out, gets tragic in the personal...'

'It's trivial,' Jean-Luc says. 'Last century. Besides – Solène – she isn't mute, she's dumb. When all's revealed, she has to do her aria, cold. That's a crap trick, a lousy part. My big idea, the New America – is good!'

'The tragedy,' Sami says, 'is you, Jean-Luc. You're unconnected. No faith, no family, no place.'

'Maybe,' says Jean-Luc, 'but the time is mine. My century. You're always older than me, Sami. You are my grandfather.'

★

'We were on the edge, Jean-Luc,' says Mélusine. 'Resolving something. We were close...'

'We're still falling, Mélusine,' Jean-Luc says.

★

In the country, there's real colours. No picture gallery.
Without frames and silences, without a sleeping guardian.
Smells, real chemicals, true fouled water. Birds armed only
with a claw, a beak...

There's always games, fun for the family, after the arts,
the martial kind ... games grand, unticketed, unbounded –
a scrum they call *bouchkazi*, on little horses, no one dies,
except the goat, decapitated – *ulag* is its name.

The game – it comes from somewhere far away, all shout
and hustle in – it's like the play of tiger cubs ... imported,
like those Parthian bows ... a super-springiness ...
slingshots and javelins too... Those guys, lurking in the
woods – maybe they've practised, perfect: waiting for our
guys.

To play, you need the horse – it should be yours, to fit...
Or – there's poetry – a prize for off-the-cuff... There, love
still plays the fool, the dog-rose blooms, your girl goes with
the gypsies – you only get one bite at anything, bobbing for
apples in the barrel...the water's thick as spit.

Wooden saddles – they make them here. Their speciality.

The hut that burned, the still exploded – where Ali died,
prayed: all started small. Now I live there, it's got large. Of
course, some rooms you don't go in, some space is burnt to
nothing – there's a big hall, wooden chairs set against the
wall, a brigands' space-ship, I'm the bottled foetus on the
mantle.

The horses – they aren't shod – they're playing on the
grass, a piece of grassland steppe abutting on to silvery

trees: behind them the tall pines, bare up their brown thighs, and then their green topknots...

'What are you waiting for?' Lénick asks me. 'Directions? You're flimsy, like the plastic discs they throw...'

'I'm checking on the damage, Lénick,' I say. 'Reporting the wars. The deprivation.'

We're neighbours, Lénick, I...

'I already have a girl,' I say. 'Lighter than air, she is, lighter than me.'

'Well, good for you,' she says. 'I don't see anyone else around... If your cash won't come, and you don't play – you have to bet. That's it! That's what you do.'

'You're a country girl, Lénick,' I say. 'You think in stereotypes. I could win at *bouchkazi* – those martial arts, they don't attract...'

'You idiot,' she says. '*Bouchkazi* – that's the most martial of them all. But – my aunt, Gisèle, she'll take your bet. And if you win, you'll buy the horse she's lent...'

It's not so difficult. My horse is small and weak, it penetrates the throng – my! this goat is heavy, even without its head...You pluck it off the ground, tie it to the saddle-bow. The sport goes on for days, and there's no bounds, there's many winners, many rounds – but this time, I secure the goat – weighs like a pig of iron – and go beyond the boundary, I ride, ride on, into the trees – there's no gangs hidden there that I can see, but many shacks and huts, burnt down, and boughs piled up – for charcoal, then abandoned. It's a ruined place, for sure...

Gisèle pays up: money for life: it doesn't last. The warriors avoid me, Lénick is demanding, while I wait for dear Solène – Lénick comes in with me, her aunt can't stand us near, after my winnings broke her book... That family's all coloured up, religious freaks no doubt ... dancing and painted faces...

'Where did you leave the goat?' asks Lénick. 'You're supposed to bring it back.'

'Amanda?' I ask Lénick. 'Tell me...'

'Oh we all know that,' she says.

They all know different. Sex with the wrong guy, too zealous when she's mayor – there is no mystery, there's foundation myths – the child forsaken, who'll return ... conflicts between here and there... Those rites... Spring festival – *Navroz* – anyone can snatch your girl, your land, some tradition in from somewhere else...

'Don't give your cash to your mad friend, Jean-Luc,' says Lénick. 'If you report on us, the village, the emergency – tell him it's all a movie ... everything we do... Tell him the wars will last for thirty, or a hundred years, everywhere there's devastation... Then it all turns back, goes good.'

'I've done that, Lénick. Maybe he's already changed his tack,' I say. 'Besides, his brain was cleared of movies – he's a city guy. They like things straight, along the line... That's how you change the world...'

This country life – it makes you doubt. Solène – ah, dear Solène – she's just a body now, a blossom, white as spring. But – those city vows don't mean a thing. Here in the country, here ... you're made to pay for breaking words ... best not to speak.

'I must go back,' I say. 'The escapees...'

'Now you're one of them, an escapee,' Lénick says. 'And no one ever leaves – they move around. Any one of us could be the forsaken child – or be the one forsaking. If the prodigal returns – do we rejoice or fight? Remember what they sing: "God is gone up with a shout..." People say they hear it, after the shout: "the Lord most high is terrible..." That I can believe.'

'Believe, Lénick?'I ask, bemused.

'Nothing costs nothing,' says Lénick. 'I believe you should do some work – my culture's definite about that. You could make charcoal. You'd be black. No one would cuddle you. You never sleep while it is smouldering – if you do, it burns, burns all the trees, and then the grass, and then ... you hear it.'

'That's what it means – "God, with a shout..."' I say

'If you like,' says Lénick. 'Not God, though – it's us! Burning.'

'That might be the choice you've made,' I say.

She stares at me: 'If I'm in the wood,' I say. 'Burning the trees to make them burn again, a black imp on my cone – I'm the sentinel. That's not safe. Best keep schtum, when you see the guys come, and watch them from the trees.'

She nods. 'You'd all do better playing less,' I say. 'Start growing flowers. There's conferences and opera too, and funerals...'

'Oh yes?' says Lénick, laughing. 'You'll tell us how to do our farming, now you've spoiled the game and hid the goat?'

We laugh.

There, the matter rests.

★

'Make them all sing, Sami,' says Karlheinz. 'That's all it takes – in turn, to make a show. Then go round, take their orders – booze and pills, I know how backstage works. You're author and servant, you write the words, do the emotions, feed the weaknesses.'

'I see you've never seen a show,' says Sami. 'Though it may be, you and I – our time will come...'

'Don't bet on it,' Jean-Luc says. 'You're both the flim-flam man – flim, not film, I emphasise. I've no use for either of you: science. That's my new concern. These discoveries ... is there an order? Is what we discover *there*, always, from the start? Like opening parcels, eating the hard-boiled eggs...Are some things easier than others, that they come first to those? Is there an end point? Why is it there, who set it up – the things science says it finds...?'

'It's secrets in a garden – that's the biggest secret of them all,' says Solène, leaning on her broom. 'A garden – why?' She's seldom spoken out before –

'Look at the screen,' Jean-Luc says, ignoring her. The TV's always on, dropping its conceits. 'The sex lives of green iguanas. Who's the dominant male round here? Who do I fight? Some grey sacklike crook, keeps seven wives behind the panelling...'

'Maybe it's the other kind,' says Karlheinz. 'Mélusine – the spindly leggy brute who feasts on us...'

'That scene is closed,' Jean-Luc says. 'That's nature – we got on top of that. The challenge now – is ethics. My idea is this: justice... Everybody says it comes too late, that guys have died long, long before they saw the transformation, set straight their lives... Justice arrives too late, if it arrives at all. Science – quite unpredictable, most often useless, arcane stuff. Put them together... How? Living longer, that's the answer. Working less or not at all – we'll sell resources, sit in our chair ... the war will end, the grass turn green, the poet find her rhyme...'

'Wise Georgians...' says Karlheinz. 'Could be us! Forget your birthdate, live for centuries... Jean-Luc, you're quite played out!'

'Think iguanas. Tortoises,' Jean-Luc says. 'They don't work – they eat and screw. They live. We could too – and better. We've entertainment. It's distribution, Karlheinz, that's the nub – to each their patch, their ration. I'll work something out.'

'This scheme's more pathetic than the last, Jean-Luc,' says Mélusine. 'What's more, I'm tired of all these people dropping in to eat, people you don't know, and I don't want to...'

'Mélusine,' says Jean-Luc, irritated. 'Solène does all the catering, and you have missed the point. Long life. What does it entail? Think, you sceptics! First – justice. Then – food. Equality.'

'I can't promote all that,' says Mélusine. 'People here just pig their food and hope it doesn't make them fat. People elsewhere – they have equality: it's killing them. They scrabble in the dust ... achieving some inequality, that's their salvation, their great hope...'

'You haven't understood at all. People want their immortality right now,' Jean-Luc says. 'If you fear for our eternity, you daren't oppress, provoke – it might bring on your death... From this, all else will follow on...'

'No, Jean-Luc,' Karlheinz says. 'This time, you've oversimplified – deceived as well.'

★

'I've just found out,' says Sami, quite distraught, 'I have an illness. It's been diagnosed – a condition, as they say "unknown to science". What does that presage...? You've all been chatting on that brink...'

'I think you've guessed how it scrolls out,' says Jean-Luc. 'But – the concept's fascinating. Something unknown to science, outside the frontier... A thing beyond; beyond hypothesis, beyond a cure, a palliative – no label and no drawer... At last! An unknown, bearing worlds unknown...'

'Maybe it's a miracle,' says Solène.

'Now this!' shouts Mélusine. 'A terminal condition, on top of Jean-Luc's crap campaign – I'll have no hand in it. Back to the fundamentals, all of you! The kitchen and the supermart – prepare to study those! Those are our continuity...'

'I see that I was right,' says Jean-Luc. 'Sami – you're on the way to your non-being, as I theorised before. What will you make of it? Not much, I'd guess, seeing how you waste your time, hanging round us here...'

'I expected more than this, my friends,' says Sami, weeping, angry too: 'Your stuff, Jean-Luc – it's vulgar pep: "Get out your chair and write your name upon the wall..." Even if the wall falls down, or vengeance makes you strike – Amanda, in this case. What if we all did this – pursued our interest and our will to happiness … ending in battles, massacres.'

'You've got it wrong,' Jean-Luc says. 'I'm not responsible for accidents.'

'They all say that,' says Mélusine.

'I love you, Sami,' says Soléne. 'I always have. I'll carry you, and place you in the boat and pay the boatman, if I can...'

'That's quite a turn,' says Sami, looking sour. 'I'm motionless, I've quite seized up – though how you'll care for me, Solène, when we don't know what my affliction is, I can't conceive.'

'That guy, back there,' Jean-Luc says, remembering me, the village, the disciplines, manoeuvres without end. 'He can forget writing his report. Destruction starts and ends, just like its twin. Creation. And as for you,' he glares around. 'Vulgarisers, philistines! Read my book! It's not about a choice, a choice to choose, or not. Sami here, he has no choice! His boss is death! But – he can live the good life now... The good life – has no start, no term. It's good, that's all.'

'They'll never do my opera,' Sami complains. 'See how the plot is chewing at its tail...'

'We never thought it had a chance,' says Mélusine.

'That's exactly my philosophy,' Jean-Luc says. 'Sami – an escapee. Like the rest – his house, his future – tumbled down: a human earthquake. An accident, caused by others, quite beyond the reach of vengeance. Philosophy teaches you – first, you run. Then, you seek significance. Good life. In your case, Sami, a woman, adoration not reciprocated, who is not your type – sacrifices herself for you. That's good

– better than for most of us. The good life – it's underneath the happenstance, the weaknesses, lack of desires ... but – there it is! An idea for your opera: – quite grotesque: a melodrama without tears, the final aria – happiness!'

'Don't listen, Sami,' says Solène. 'I'm your princess, the sweetness in the fruit...'

'There, Sami,' says Mélusine. 'Make it comic. Sparkle!'

'Remember,' Sami says, 'there's no words or music yet – it's just how things unroll.'

'Oh comic, absolutely,' says Mélusine, locking her bedroom door from the outside. 'Off limits! Sami can lie on cushions in the vestibule, Solène. I must have my privacy. When I think – our grandfathers had the cultural revolution. Hear the echoes, our ancestors' great leaps, the pratfalls and the cries! We only have disorders – elderly, newly infantile, unscientific and obsessive. Oh! I could cry along with Sami. Not that he knows what tears are for... They're for the past that really was – not for what might have been, and wasn't.'

'I'm back in jail,' says Sami. 'My body. My bones are window bars. This time, I don't want to leave.'

'What were you in for, Sami?' Karlheinz asks. 'Nothing minor, unromantic, that's the hope. Once for life, and now for death. It seems before, you had a window too!'

But Sami groans – the neighbours turn their music up, shout from the atrium, complain.

★

'We thrash, Jean-Luc,' says Mélusine. 'We've made the net that's caught us. We say we're threatened, say we're poor. We're safe. We're comfortable... We support the people – the people, they support us. Out in the villages – that's the front line. Who's the enemy? Gangs in the woods? Perhaps. Sometimes, those village guys, they suffer. Beyond the normal. Things obscure and unexplained...'

'We can't give up, Mélusine,' Jean-Luc says. 'Not even now. We are the good. What if everyone like us gave up everything?'

'There's only one of us,' says Mélusine. 'We're all the same. Informed. Futility. Others less smart – doing what we hope to do, with more effect. Or none.'

'I can take you where it's more intense...' Karlheinz says. 'Sami – he understands form. He's fiddled with the changing scenes, villains, heroes, turn and turnabout. Form above all else. His pain – will end with clash of swords, a rataplan of spear-butts... "How'll we go on tomorrow night, without the hero?" There's the applause ... sorrow? Glad it's finished? A crepitation in the air – is that reward?'

'Solène, Solène,' shouts Sami. 'It's going dark. Canaries – maybe in the black they cannot see to sing, and there's no prompt ... is this the way, the avant-garde ... oh, lead me...? This beige air – I can't get it down me...'

'She loves you, Sami,' says Jean-Luc. 'It doesn't mean she'll come to you because you shout.'

'Solàne!' he shouts.

'It's dark for everyone, not just for you,' says Mélusine. 'The end – it takes no special skill, or even literacy, to execute. Just wait. It comes.'

*

Vito's the boss. He has ambitions too – most undeclared.

'What's here?' asks Mélusine, flustered. 'Who's in charge? And where's the centre?'

'There's places for you in the wood,' says Karlheinz. 'Food, the right time, who to pay – I'll mediate it for you. Give me the cash... Who wants to sleep with who?'

'Where's Solène?' I ask.

'You here still?' Jean-Luc asks. 'She's in love. She's finishing off a comedy, she'll turn it into tragedy.'

'I can't stay here,' says Mélusine. 'I can't speak with Vito. Sylvain's worse. Someone must have responsibility, a plan... Jean-Luc! – here may be more intense – but it's collapsed. There's people come from everywhere – what happens to the places they have left – without their arms and legs ... how'll they walk and carry, hoe and dig?'

'It's you, Mélusine,' Jean-Luc says. 'You're lost without a power to chat to – you say you subvert and criticise – but really you collude. You lick power's polished shoe.'

'Karlheinz should sell them arms,' says Mélusine, desperately. 'But will they then attack? Defend? And who, and who?'

'When this guy's dead, Solène will come?' I ask – it could be difficult ... there's Lénick...

'Oh no,' says Mélusine. 'She's not an escapee: she's settled there, where there'll be nothing left for her... And mothers die, you know – it's not a mystery, Amanda? Leave that, beneath its stone.'

'There can't be planning here, no big idea,' says Jean-Luc, 'People just come in and out, and then they settle, or they leave. Solène's mother was the mayor – remember, Mélusine? You could have talked with her, the boss...'

'Vito has plans...' Karlheinz begins, 'But you won't like the way he sees you fitting in...'

'Amanda – when she went, the balance went with her...' says Mélusine. 'People like a movement, one that rolls ... they like feeling good. Feeling good's as good as being good. Your troubles justify resentment, the anger that you feel. Amanda couldn't face all that. She has no legacy. Look how Solène's turned out! She's not dynastic, that's for sure...'

'These games get on my nerves,' says Jean-Luc. 'I wanted discipline: all that's come out is warriors...'

'I saw Vito,' Karlheinz says. 'He says, "I can be anything, any sex or none, religion – none. Color, place... Hunan? You want that? Yes, I can be from there. It's ridiculous, the reactionary stuff, its expectations, you guys lost in it... I'm on fire," says Vito ... "I'll show you what you couldn't dream..."'

'It's obvious,' Jean-Luc says. 'Thousands of years, nothing resolved, the same old chatter, massacres the same. Black, white, men, women, us, strangers... So, what's Vito got that's new? Another jacquerie?'

'I think that's just Karlheinz talking,' says Mélusine. 'Not Vito. Surprise me more! Conjure something up – that dull guy we dumped here – he won the goat game! Here, yes, it's more intense – but useless too, illegible. Now, I must get sorted out. Into the trees...'

Here's the ruins. Mysteries everywhere, even in ruins – forget them, pass it over.

Further in ... a mansion, like on a plantation... People laden, running in and out.

'This must be for me,' thinks Mélusine.

There's baskets, borne by domestics on the scurry, full of mangos, large as brown heads with rosy cheeks, and smells of fenugreek and capsicum – no flesh, no feathers, but striped seeds – must be for the parrots hung in cages – now she sees – no bars, no locks on the bars, just a perch, a bath – the mansion's facade seems Mughal, those red green lozenges, though ... the tall teak timbers in the loggia floated up ... doors that slide and doors that aren't, just walls...

'Certainly, it's for me,' says Mélusine. 'I'll move right in, put a lock on everything, plants for my salon...' 'Do I have to pay the servitù?' she asks a guy with piping down his pants... She calls him Whistler, that's what he does – air always out his embouchure, pinched like for a kiss...

'Oh no,' he says. 'This mansion – does not exist. It's built of air, and if you ask too much, it all folds up, we tuck it in our belt, and us, we waft away...'

'You mean,' says Mélusine, starting a tear, 'I can't live here?'

'Of course you can. You musn't ask to pay. You musn't lock it up. Just keep schtum. Enjoy: enjoy your stay,' says the guy.

'Oh no,' says Mélusine. 'It's too good to be true.'

'It is,' the guy says, laughs. 'That would be fantasy, if it were true. So – it's not.'

'You country guys,' says Mélusine. 'I know – you live in a place were we logicians cannot go – the festivals, the masks ... the seeds that turn to beans, so high they overtop the castle walls, I know, this is your universe ... the stars unnamed, the moon that sings a song... You manage all this stuff until there's floods, a storm that blows it all away, the trees that turn to torches...'

'Yes, yes,' the guy says. 'All of that. We can sing, and we can dance. You, Mélusine, must just keep quiet. Live here, ask nothing, pick the persimons, pour your gin yourself, don't sleep on sheets, we don't do laundry here...'

'Tell me the secret. Now!' says Mélusine.

'Our mayor,' the guy says, yielding at once to Mélusine. 'She built it for herself. She is no more. Maybe a moralist – had punished her. Or wanted it himself...'

'Were there no relatives?' asks Mélusine. 'A daughter, say?'

'You mustn't spoil your kids,' says the guy, choosing a fruit and sucking it. 'Solène was made for love, and not embezzlement. She lived once in the official hut. She'll not be back.'

'It's so,' says Mélusine. 'There's opportunities in town you don't find here. They say love's a garden: plants – they grow too tall. Or else they die. Solène's love is dying. It all does. How deep the roots are buried, like Ali's here, in the dark earth! Twined in the bones.'

'Oh see how many gardens we have here,' says Whistler. 'Hear the grackles in the cypresses, the air's tuned like a string...'

'I bet there's chapels here, and temples underground,' says Mélusine.

'You'll learn the place – nothing is built by chance – there's maths and lessons to be learnt, and rocks to carve with diamond drills, the soil's imported – river silt from the Amur, with stones like catseyes,' Whistler says.

★

'I'm lodged deep inside,' Mélusine tells Jean-Luc. 'The wood. Find your own space, Jean-Luc. I'm in a witches' hut – she stacks me with her brooms.' They laugh.

In the mansion, Mélusine does well – no one speaks to anyone, but she is top – they all defer to her, for being smart, and talking down to powerful guys.

'I'm in Vito's old shebeen,' says Jean-Luc. 'Karlheinz has a sentry box – a lookout for Vito's guys...'

They all do better than they say – but Mélusine lives like a princess of the steppe, she doesn't need to hunt, or milk the goats, or make the apple marmalade, nor turn the cheeses...

Vito's built a guardhouse – he has in mind an exploit: no massacres, no expeditions like all those before...

★

Whistler – the air comes out of him the colour of the tunes – it could be irritating, the whistling, but for Mélusine, the terms of lodging are so favourable, she tolerates. She wanders in the gardens – there's Dutch, French, Italian, a wilderness, a kitchen – and a maze... 'Love,' she tells Whistler. 'I'm not a stranger to it. It's brittle – all the many

I've endured, planted, watered with my tears or someone else's... It dies, or else it grows so tall, you have to cut its head off... I prefer – all that is solid. Love – it's the will. It bends, it snaps. Soft as honey-wax. Real power – has interest. That bears it up. It rests on real things, real people. Like – where does Vito's money come from, Whistler? Not from the hospice work, not from the medicines he sells... Real money, Whistler...'

'That's your province, Mélusine,' says Whistler. 'There's a picture called "Death of the Miser" – that's how they saw it, the imps and demons round like cockroaches, a death well merited... No power without money, Mélusine, however bad a name it has. Money's there to spend, the lesson's clear. Better spend everything, die poor, Mélusine, than have the devil round your bed.'

'I see Vito in the role,' says Mélusine. 'Imp. Devil. His iron stave ... all that. Finishing the suffering...'

'There's a hanging garden too,' says Whistler. 'Not used much these days. Shed no blood – remember the book... See –' and he points to high ripple-walls enclosing – 'That's design!' he says. 'You can't see in from mansion windows. That's where we burn the halms...'

'There must be beds of mandrakes there,' says Mélusine. 'That's where power lay, did its business. Drew the line – guilt, innocence, hohum. The nuisances, and all the rest – like cockroaches. Not my view, of course, but it's culture, history. Sometimes – you have to forget about it. The hanging garden, by the brook. If there's not a drop, you get a moment of euphoria, not that anyone has left descriptions... The singing of the birds, the cool blue air beneath your bare feet...'

'In those days,' says Whistler. 'It was all laid down. Choice – and order. Choosing sides, submitting to an order. Now, there's Vito. His rules, his order. But the hanging garden's fallen into ruin – there's not the thirst for ceremony...'

'Here you have no private place,' says Mélusine, 'there's no locks on the doors – how do you manage sex? Or are you all too busy, scurrying with baskets...'

'Of course,' says Whistler, 'there's abundant other things to do. It doesn't last for long, at any rate, the act: and we don't procreate. Love's better in the head than in the groin, don't you agree?'

'Oh yes,' says Mélusine. 'Men go on about it lots – I found I didn't like the hunt – the running! Exhausting, and those lolling tongues, the whooping horns! And even worse, perhaps – the guys that caught me – didn't much enjoy! They said they would, they said they had – all lies! The moment passed in tempest, sea-drift, then rotten timbers on the beach...'

Mélusine and Whistler walk round, arm in arm – each has a basket, in go leaves and mushrooms, roots and seeds. Jean-Luc is far away, body and spirit...

*

Karlheinz says to me, 'Despots. Families, clans, religious freaks. Then came trade, elected thieves – Amanda... Money came to her, and some went on to Vito. He must do something with it...'

'I know all that, Karlheinz,' I say. 'Solène does penance for it, for the fires. Maybe it is best she stays in town... Lénick tells me everything. Where do I come in? What do you want, Karlheinz? I could show you how to ride, win at bou*chkazi* – I know a horse that suits, and I'll take cash.'

'Riding, eh?' Karlheinz says, looks uncomfortable. 'That sounds quite a complicated thing – the different speeds, all that, stop start and whoa, and what the horse decides...'

'Well,' I say, 'you can complicate it so, I guess. I do it just by sitting there and steering it, and making it go fast until it tires.'

'Suppose I win,' Karlheinz says. 'What you call bou*chkazi*. What then?'

'You wouldn't need do it twice,' I say. 'I don't. Nor even once. You sneak in alone, honour the goat, lift it up and bury it.'

'That doesn't sound the spirit of the thing,' he says.

We leave it there.

*

'This business of the horse,' says Jean-Luc. 'It's interesting – more interesting than where I try to sleep and there is roistering. All hours, most volumes. The centaur – has a tenderness, naivety, where you would think it's smarter, quicker, than mere horse, mere man. It's not just brash... Solène tells me – Sami's lost his grip, his sense of time. That's not unknown to science, that affliction – it's that science doesn't know wherein the answer lies – on the blackboard, in black holes,' and he laughs, pleased with himself. 'How does time unroll, smooth like oil, or shaped like tessera, those biscuits made for alphabet soup...? And where does history fit in? Is that our part of viscous time, we freeze it, make it aspic? How could we do without it – time, our time, time past? How does time leave behind what it does, goes on, then there's something new? Time – the sculptor? The exterminator? The question Sami asks is "Do I want immortality? or eternal life?" Wanting: that too is interesting ... it isn't in the maths, or in the stars... Immortality: you could be a virus in a vault. Eternal life – is riding on your Harley – all that road, and those motels...

'Sami has a point. When you are coming to an end, and time's not going on for you, you think: "there – it's over", but actually, it's going on, and history too, its footfalls heavier – you've footholds both in time and history, let's say – you think of where you stood, you contemplate the reel of different things, mostly unseen, that pass by while you are being your unique self, doing your five-a-day, abhorring heresy, having doubts, and drinking tea ... doing time in jail, or in the cave of sleep...'

'Sami's finished, then?' asks Karlheinz: 'Solène will come...'

'Sami doesn't understand if he's moving slow, or very fast. We know – he's nearly stopped,' Jean-Luc says, 'but it's a labyrinth he's in – it has a heart, a centre. When you reach it – have you won the game? Or lost? Have you found? – or are you most completely gone...? It's empty, that's for sure.'

'This here is not the place to ask,' says Karlheinz, who doesn't understand, and doesn't care. 'It's true – time is of interest to rocks and rocketeers. Our interest's in history. Sami – well, his history was his opera, his place, his time,

celebrity – we knew about it, though it didn't quite exist...
And now – he's no idea where he is. No place or time to
hold to. Otherwise, he's fine. Solène won't come, won't
leave him.'

'You can't get far without a theory of time,' Jean-Luc
says. 'It isn't easy, if your maths is weak...'

'We've no money, Jean-Luc,' Karlheinz says. 'I'm always
on sentry fatigue – I never sleep, so I can't figure out a scam,
a business model, as they say...'

I'm relieved. Of course, I love Solène – but love's the
same, wherever she is, or I am.

Lénick talks incessantly. 'I'm getting big,' she says to me,
'You're getting thin. It ends that I shall eat you up...'

I say, 'Vito's not trustworthy, Lénick. He has guards – if
you're one of those, you have to circle round, dance, change
your name, put on an accent...'

'Surely you could do the accent,' Lénick says. 'It's for
security, of course. And cash...'

'I need to know – security for who? From who?' I say.
'Defence – or may it be attack? Being paranoid is not
enough – day and night, guys you don't know – they want
on principle to see you dead.'

'Oh, faddle!' Lénick says. 'Vito's a hedgehog – spikes all
round. Remember Bonaparte!'

'He does,' I say.

'Win at *bouchkazi* then,' she says. 'Or whatever it is
called.'

'I don't like you, Lénick,' I tell her.

'You don't understand the culture here,' she says. 'You
don't have to like me, or anyone.'

*

'Mushrooms,' shouts Mélusine. 'That's it! I'm dying, Whistler.'

'Oh no!' says Whistler. 'You were wrong! We don't eat that stuff! It's all for show. We pluck it from the ground – that's full of worms and who knows what – chemicals, no doubt... You're lucky, Mélusine. No one can die here, in the mansion – Vito, the ambassadors – his team that put you down when that time comes, the cart, the carpenter, the raven with the bell, the flight of swans, the skiff, the water that you don't remember if you've drowned in it... No death here, not in the mansion! Imagine – how hard it is, to keep a death a secret – and the corpse! I suppose, dear Mélusine, you'd put it in the rhubarb patch, and then complain when you'd consumed the pie: of course, you'd have its pain, transmitted through a tuber. You notice – how it's passed, from parents on, their children, at their birth – no good fairy at the crib – then on and on – death is a catching thing, and if you garden, farm and harvest it ... it feeds and feeds...'

'I'm sure to live,' says Mélusine resisting her malaise. 'But, I'll crawl to the village, to my old friends, not disturbing you... Whistler! – I'll be back.'

*

'I'm dying, Jean-Luc,' says Mélusine, scrabbling on the floor. Amanda died here, there's the glass from Vito's broken spirits all around... 'But my time – it isn't right.'

'The time – it's quite indifferent. But where you stand, how fast you're travelling, it may count – maybe if you're behind the curve, you beat your destiny. Remember, if the time is right – it will also be the place that's right,' says Jean-Luc. 'It's a big idea – but nothing can be done with it.'

'Those maroon mushrooms, someone should label them,' says Mélusine.

They celebrate. Jean-Luc warns Mélusine – Beware the coloured things, beware the poisoned air, the smoke, the mists, miasmas...

'Mélusine,' Jean-Luc says. 'Just the sickness? Those toadstools gave you nothing more? Effects that we could publicise, maybe, and market too?'

'Oh, Jean-Luc,' says Mélusine, 'how you disappoint me! Well, of course, the visions – those, I've always had,' and she shapes a castle in the air, quite like her current home. She fears her mansion, homestead, might just disappear – ejected into nowhere by some potent sphincter, expelling dear Whistler too ... weeds invade and make the gardens one dense canvas ... arsenic green...

'The thing is, Mélusine,' Jean-Luc says, 'I'm out of cash. How to articulate a plan to captivate the yokels here?'

'You're living in Amanda's place that burned,' says Mélusine. 'You did her wrong, I bet.'

'People must look out for themselves,' Jean-Luc says. 'Don't keep munitions underneath your bed.'

'Talk to Vito, Jean-Luc. Don't sign up to join his guard. Give him a big idea,' she says.

She runs back through the woods. It's there! The barley-sugar twisted chimneys; stucco like green marzipan; the bryony along the path; the ballerinas rocking on the porch...

'Oh Whistler, those goddam *funghi* – I see it all, so clear – except...' and she weeps, poor Mélusine. 'I used to see the present. Now, I see the past of everything – there's a caul, a cloak, a web ... there is the tree in bloom – but I can see the buds, the winter boughs, the sapling, and the root... When I look at Whistler – you're a joyous spermatozoon, then bound into the stroller, now you're struggling with the alphabet ... all is layered on...'

'We all knew that,' says Whistler, quite put out. 'It sounds banal. You only see what is, of course, or what has been. The real trick would be to see the future – useful at the track, or at the cards...'

'It's true, dear Whistler. The future – hmmm – that's gone by somewhere so quick that you won't catch it up,' says Mélusine. 'It's those mushrooms ... maybe more vodka... About the alphabet, dear Whistler – it still troubles you, I bet.'

'No, not at all,' he says. 'We don't read or write – it brings you troubles greater than they could resolve.'

'Your ignorance brings wisdom, Whistler,' says Mélusine. 'And you distil a mighty vodka here... I feel...'

'Oh, states of mind, poohpooh,' laughs Whistler. 'Once you've experienced one bizarre condition, maybe hallucinations – repetition is superfluous: a slippery ride.'

*

'Food, Sami?' Solène asks. 'Are you ready?'

'No, my dear,' says Sami. 'It's been years. Eating doesn't belong. Not yet.'

'Oh, it's not been that long,' says Solène, stroking his face.

★

'Every village,' says Karlheinz, 'has its militia.'

'It's true,' Jean-Luc says. 'The Arabs, the Bosniaks – they have militias. We have Vito. You must be loyal to him, and all the rest that's with you. Like the Panthers, the Resistance – everywhere, all over – there's militias. Who says Vito isn't good for a spin? You can bet – if they're everywhere, militias, we need one too.'

'That's right, Jean-Luc,' says Karlheinz. 'When we have one going – there'll be cash. You need good stuff for your kitbags, you're facing pros.'

'You must be already mustered, Karlheinz,' I say. 'To have the sentry-box to sleep in.'

'No, no,' says Karlheinz. 'I only took the oath. I don't have boots, or anything, I can't do deals – the box is theirs – I've nothing of my own.'

'It's true for all of us, we've nothing to defend,' Jean-Luc says. 'And where is Mélusine? She can sniff out the biggest cheese, and cut her wedge from them...'

We drink, we shout, just like real soldiers do.

'I'll go along with you,' says Jean-Luc. 'To arms, citizens! and escapees!'

'You're the one who ought to join,' says Karlheinz, pinching my arm. 'You've affective relations hereabouts...'

'To please Lénick?' I ask. 'Save her from dishonour? I'm not your man for that.'

We leave it there, but we'll be back to it.

*

'Each summer,' Whistler says to Mélusine. 'We do a masque. The solstice. Each is anonymous – we all wear masks, the sun, the moon, the night, love and repentance. No one will speak, but at the end, there's those two peacocks – they weave around, making their noise, and at the dawn – we roast them. It's a luxury we only concede ourselves, once every year.'

'They'll make the rose,' says Mélusine. 'Just like real men.'

'Oh,' says Whistler, 'of course: they know. Or else it wouldn't be quite fair, and they might fail to do a perfect show. They're proud. It's their tradition – egg after perfect egg, the family – that is their destiny, the feast. They are convinced of it – so, what else can you do?'

'No music, then,' says Mélusine. 'There's often some allegory, a classic show...'

'Like Penthesilea?' asks Whistler. 'That didn't mean so much.'

He's serious about the ceremony. He takes his costume from its bag.

'Oh Whistler – your red suit – my! how it's you, the real you... I hope you're not the devil?' and she laughs.

'I am the flame,' says Whistler.

'Not threatening the place, the estate, so quiet, so secret, so precarious?' asks Mélusine.

'We must show the risk,' says Whistler. 'Of losing it. Setting the fire. When I'm the flame – they're safe, but on the brink. Silent through the trees I run, the pines so high, like monstrous vestas...'

'I should have a part,' says Mélusine. 'Like – I could be a queen.'

'No,' says Whistler. 'Here – I am the queen.'

They watch the women paring down the grass with silent scissors ... everything is grey as air – the smoke that rises from the charcoal pans.

'Two peacocks only – hardly enough for each to get a taste,' says Mélusine, taking on the spirit...

'Oh, hardly that, dear Mélusine. The masque is not to stuff, to eat, have sex. We don't consume the precious dears – oh no! We don't become their flesh, nor they are us! We celebrate our non-existence here – we are the hidden ones – returned, but no one knows. The great return – it's true. It's never permanent, it's always followed by new disappearance. You are the grandest presence here, dear Mélusine,' says Whistler. 'But you don't figure in the masque. That is for us. And you – aren't one of us.'

'And yet,' says Mélusine. 'This camp, plantation – improvised and quiet – how it attracts me! How it makes my past a waste: Jean-Luc, the chatting to those awful painters, the diplomats, the guys who think they are the Fates – my! it disgusts me, Whistler.'

'You've made a sheaf of problems for yourself, poor Mélusine,' says Whistler. 'We have only one. Not to be discovered, not to be revealed, transferred, demolished, or imprisoned ... just Glamrock, and starlets twinkling with welcome and desire... The revelation, the dance, the dark: but always masked.'

'Don't, Whistler, don't!' says Mélusine. 'Stay where you are. Here there is plenty – there, beyond the planet's curvature, there's misery and disillusion. I know – I come from there...'

'Oh,' says Whistler. 'I think deep down we know we shall be disappointed. But – this place is quite ephemeral. You can't stay here – the fire will come, the soldiers too...'

'Oh,' says Mélusine. 'I shall keep quiet, you bet.'

★

'Try swallowing this pill, Sami,' says Solène. 'There's nothing else...'

'Aida trumpets, Solène,' Sami says. 'We used to have a set...'

'Oh you'll hear those, for sure,' she says. 'And walk among the palmtrees, see the river... You can lie here in my arms for years... It's not a cure, but there is nothing else, the scene is fixed, there are no ropes, nothing revolves, there is no other setting possible – your eyes are filled only with the picture that you've made...'

'It's all I want, Solène,' he says.

★

'And at the end, they leave?' says Mélusine. 'No, it can't be so. A masque ... it celebrates, nothing is resolved: what is, is glorified.'

The residents – they're trying on their masks – all have the mouth, a hole, the same, conveying hope, despair, it could be contemptuous. Or indifferent. The sun, the moon, those faces lead you on. A kiss? Why not? The mouth, fixed – no invitation, nothing is refused. No tongue intrudes on you, extrudes – can pass between those golden lips. What makes them moving so, there's just the frozen face? The body – it adds nothing... Men and women in the moon. They're in a place not yours! It's theirs! Keep off!

All night the icy faces nod and pass. Mélusine – she doesn't know them, unmasked, they never speak to her, now they look up – the dark sky ... the angry and the sad – linking arms in threes and fours, turning roundabout. Behind, the sightless mansion, in front – the trees, a rampart.

Then Whistler does his turn – runs, a single flame, into the rustling black. A harbinger, a fox, his tail an ember – fleeing a nothing, trying to outrun. Whistler bears a story, to and fro he races – the rest look on – each sentiment plastered on, life learned from a pattern-book.

Then – they're all gone. It's over. The peacocks – there's their flame-resistant feet and frizzled tails ... over too for them.

'What next?' asks Mélusine. 'What can I do now?'

It's dark, the mansion's – over there? The walls of the hanging garden are so high – you can't see its outline. If there'd been fireworks – but of course you can't. Those rockets – once they were ladders in the sky, now, there's only forbidding places, people exploding in the streets, or where you mustn't go, where it's not yours at all – the moon.

Underfoot, there's rubbish, tarpaulins, white enamel bowls... She skirts Jean-Luc's tumbledown. There's an owl,

you didn't see – and there's a tree, you didn't see that either
... ouch!

★

'Halt!' It's Karlheinz, can't sleep, cold in his box, the watch
– the watch on the Rhine, she thinks, the desert of the
Tatars...

'Mélusine!' he says. 'Where've you been? Among the
escapees?'

'I was in my hut, Karlheinz,' she says. 'It's cold for
summer. I can't light a fire.'

'No!' laughs Karlheinz. 'You'll burn us down. Instead of
water, cold and hot – there's just the air. We need to sink
some wells – the escapees can start the dig ... grow their
own food too, find a patch maybe, exotic stuff, the
turmeric, the leeks...'

'The fire's the threat,' says Mélusine. 'Because we all live
here. Then – there's the gangs – deep in the wood, but – I
didn't see a soul. What's the plan? Karlheinz – what do you
know? You're all dressed up, a little warrior, keeping us
safe, although we don't know where you are...! I stumbled
on you ... neither saw the other till we were treading on our
legs...'

'Calm, Mélusine,' Karlheinz says. 'There is no fire! Here
in my box – I've thought through everything. Waited for
who knows who to come and rip me up... All possibilities
I've pondered, ranked every one – until, here in my box,
there's only me and God. And God's responsible for
everything – and I've no blame, no sin, no sense of guilt...

I don't sleep here, stood vertical, immobile, like God, always awake, and always planning what I can resolve, the bad, the terrible, the end of innocence... And in the end – nothing's resolved, none of that my fault, for all the fault is God's...'

'They ought to let you walk about,' says Mélusine. 'Circulate. Do dodgy deals. That way, you won't obsess...'

'Why'd we need those trees?' Karlheinz asks, wildly, waving his gun. 'We need the land. The escapees, the skaps – the SKPs – they camp in there, there's ruins ... and the owls! You don't see them till it's late, and then they've gone. Burn them all down, and everything within the wood. Leave one as a monument – call it for Ali,' and he laughs.

'You're all white guys so far,' says Mélusine. 'The owls mean nothing to you, hunting up there. Enrol some skaps, broaden your minds...'

'Oh, that will come,' says Karlheinz. 'We'll negotiate with other groups – maybe we'll agree, or maybe...'

There is some hope, thinks Mélusine, the mansion is still there, perhaps, just she can't find it, see it. Better eyes, pick out more dwellings in the dark. Her home, disappeared like it was vaporised, into the dark, its population fled, deported, tufo and travertine slip into mud, the ice-cream stucco melted, the residence – loses its outline, overgrown, then crumbling into shells, becoming only time, a point observed from other points fictitious, hypothetical, the watcher of its mathematical uncertainty a spaced-out figure, one of Einstein's hundred ghosts, cutouts outposted in the universe – its wall-eyed windows blacked and shut, its wings clipped square ... an oblong learned at school containing nothing all your life, no depth, no dovetails and no lid... The masque – not "every year", never again...

'No Whistler,' says Mélusine aloud.

★

'"White" Mélusine?' Jean-Luc says. 'That's a metaphor – *your* metaphor, Mélusine.'

'We could ask Vito what it means,' says Mélusine.

'Oh, he doesn't have the time for that,' Jean-Luc says. 'Sylvain would try to tell you who he is. It'll be in vain. He speaks for Vito, they don't think much, and what they do, don't give away.'

'We came here to find things out,' says Mélusine. 'We weren't even desperate. Nor enthusiasts. And now we're caught up in it. It's serious, but if you can't recognise the threat, I guess, you must be stupid, irresponsible.'

'Everyone's caught up,' Jean-Luc says. 'Even Lénick. She talks, she gathers all the stories, they're like eggs. After months, you see which one's hatched, what kind of bird it is...'

'Lénick's not reliable,' I say. 'She doesn't have a filter – it goes in, straight out it comes...'

'Trust is difficult,' says Mélusine. 'There's boasting, especially when there's sportsmen round. No way of knowing, when it comes to muscle time.'

'I never lie,' I say.

'Oh, it isn't only you,' Jean-Luc says. 'As soon as things go bad, this crap state acts like all the rest – guys disappear, there's camps, there's prisons underground... We go along with it, so's we don't end inside...'

'Well, Jean-Luc,' says Karlheinz, with a nasty tone, 'Your theory of time. That would be important, no? Like – a theory of the lot – where we are, and where we'll end.'

'Could be, could be,' Jean-Luc says.

'Well,' says Karlheinz. 'Put things on another plane. Say I get a pleasure quite intense from torturing guys. It's pain for them. If I were to torture you to get a formula – not one I understand – would you deny me pleasure, blabbing it all out at once?'

'No, no,' Jean-Luc says. 'There's more to it than that, you're not quite understanding where you're at, the consequence...'

'Take soldiering,' Karlheinz goes on. 'There's not much pleasure there. It's not a duel, where honour is at stake. And if you have your gun, you see an enemy, unarmed, taking a leak – you shoot. A defenceless guy, quite like the innocents you're not supposed to kill – but down she goes. Painless all round, and you get a medal. Have you done good or bad?'

'You haven't got it right, Karlheinz, though I agree – those situations may occur,' Jean-Luc says, quite confident. 'If your existence is at stake – you'll do what's necessary – we suspend the right and wrong...'

'So, if we differ about time, it's quite irrelevant. The question is – am I a threat to you?' Karlheinz says. 'It's all about defending and attacking – we must start from there. It's animals, pretending to be sages...'

'Maybe it starts from there,' says Jean-Luc. 'But you argue like a pig, Karlheinz. We have a plot, scenario – call it a libretto ... the whole species does. We'll win, our side, because we're right, and have the better arms...'

'That's what Vito tells us,' says Karlheinz: 'But...'

'But nothing, Karlheinz, it's all casuistry,' says Mélusine. 'Forget the medal too.'

'What Lénick treasures,' I begin, 'is sacrosanct, of course. But Solène... I treasure her...'

'It's not your concern,' says Mélusine. 'We'd all like to live in paradise – some of us already have. Best stick to what you see, not what's hidden beyond the *place d'armes*, beyond the pines...'

⋆

This is not a kindly place. They don't treat each other with compassion. There's no way to enter in, go through those cottage doors: Lénick's sisters, you'd suppose, are closely watched and traded off. If you went in, your welcome isn't guaranteed... Don't fall off your horse. Don't have a dank or soggy brain – there's not much curing done. Don't be surprised – if Karlheinz stays, Vito survives – when they do some awful things. Some people they will save, but more they will betray. It won't be in their power, at all events – they'll do the deals, others, bigger guys, those will dispose, they'll make the casualties.

Some villages, some cities – are quite untouched. Some countries too. Maybe this little settlement will be left alone – no one could object to that. There'd be suspicion, fear, some roughing up of neighbours – nothing excessive, nothing new.

★

'We'll go back,' says Mélusine: 'You'll come,' she says to me. 'But you'll bunk up with Jean-Luc. I don't want you near, not either of you.'

I don't object, but it's not the way I'd thought...

'Karlheinz has disappointed,' Mélusine goes on. 'After all, he was a suitor. Now he thinks he's a messiah, bringing justice with his sword. Didn't you see?'

'A messiah would be awkward,' Lénick says. 'It could cause embarrassment. Does one know when one is one?'

'No,' says Mélusine, 'you know only if you're not. The idea's good, though, Lénick. You stay here and keep an eye on him.'

She shoos me off as we approach her building. 'We know how it will all turn out,' says Mélusine. 'Back there. We did our time, "the friendly lions, prowling silently around us". No harm done. Everyone's prepared. That's the snag – my job is obsolete. The powerful guys – they'll go and do where fancy takes. They pal up, or they fight – just as the idea comes to them. No mediators, no one who's read those little articles that have the vital detail... There is no hidden deep I can reveal. Before, I was a fixer, a facilitator – making a system, uncovering an interest. Now, it's charades – blindfolded, you draw the future from a hat. I'm quite superfluous. Now, off you go,' she tells Jean-Luc and me.

★

'The dry people have come back,' Solène tells Sami.

'I'm dust,' says Sami, 'I'll hide underneath a mat.'

'They say "dust" – but bones are elderberry stalks,' says Solène, who knows, being a country girl. 'You have the river damp, you're miasma.'

'They'll want to travel, start their journeys, in and out these rooms,' says Sami.

'Your life is wonderful, Sami,' Solène says. 'Always on stage, invisible – that's you, behind a rock, a waterfall ... in the boudoir, in the bower, and in the battle – you know the hero's name, who has the dagger, who's incestuous. How quickly it's all over, and you've seen it all – you don't speak, Sami, you're not messiah, but you're god impotent. Or just – an imp?'

'I've always been there, Solène,' Sami says. 'From the time they sang, and didn't need to write it down.'

'You'll die, Sami, I'll make a parcel,' says Solène. 'Then – I'm done. They'll drop you in the river; your name – no one delivers to your name. There's your wish, true.'

'I'm dying, Solène,' Sami says. 'What use are you to me? I'll be glad when I'm shot of you.'

'That's good,' Solène says. 'That's happiness.'

*

'Well, Solène,' says Mélusine, 'Sami looks dead to me. In that case, you could leave...'

'He's good,' Solène says. 'It's your problem, if he seems a corpse. His stories last such little times, all fear and frolic – and in between – there's nothing going on. He needs this couch...'

'I know all that,' says Mélusine. 'Don't play, Solène.'

'I do lose track of time, it's true,' says Sami. 'But still – we need the space, dear Mélusine.'

★

'I'm at a loss,' says Mélusine. 'There's tales of victims everywhere. No side is worth my joining it, or even smiling wanly as it flees or goes to war. My home – it should be gardens – Persian; Shiraz, maybe, for the trees. They're on a ramp, guys everywhere – to purify us, jail us, clip our wing... Too bad... Jean-Luc complains of me: my "Moderate Modernism", he says: "intolerant liberalism". Could it be, he's right?'

'You want to free those women?' Sami asks. 'Free me too.'

'Oh, they're free,' says Mélusine. 'They all read the Dream of Hafez, most are doctors of poetic arts. How they ridicule the rules! That's what I want to learn – to be like them. And think, Sami – who invented money, the lead for dogs, cages for the birds? Our ancient grandfathers! No martial arts! No formulas. No: the arts of being something else, of being where I want...'

'I wouldn't follow you, Mélusine,' says Sami. 'Low-level criminality is your consequence – hiding what you do, your cash, and what you think: smile, Mélusine, that's all you present, all that you possess... You muddle it all up. People and countries... Your wishes – they don't enter in.'

'You're formulaic, Sami – your stories – they all resolve within their time, their acts,' she says. 'Nothing dangles, nothing is uncertain – there is an end to everything – happiness, or immolation...'

'What has my death resolved?' asks Sami.

★

'Out of your depth as usual, Mélusine,' says Jean-Luc: You're soft. Leave the argument!'

'The village?' asks Mélusine. 'What we gave, what we left.'

'I don't remember anything particular,' Jean-Luc says. 'We left Karlheinz. Not much use, talking to the rest. We gave them hints – probably, the militia's on our side. Karlheinz will fight – there's a percentage for him there...'

Solène says, 'Where it all began, the civilisation. It's ending over there, perhaps it means it's ending everywhere.'

'That sounds profound, Solène,' says Mélusine. 'If I didn't know you well. That civilisation's always been a monstrous thing: what we're supposed to think is beautiful, Solène, is images staged, glimpsed through the slits placed in the barracks wall.'

Ah! Solène, I think... If only she'd let Sami drop, and show herself...

★

'I love you, Solène,' I say.

'Weren't you supposed to make charcoal?' she asks.

'It looks hard,' I say. 'When you try, it's even harder.'

'People there have everything hard,' she says. 'They're hard too. You have to forgive some strongarm – it's been done on them. Remember Saint Bartholemew? – that was just indulgence.'

'Jean-Luc tried to put a spin on it,' I say. 'But there was like a pack of dogs, and in the midst – another dog.'

'Oh,' says Solène, 'it's a smaller dog, for sure.'

'And did they spare the trees?' I ask.

'They need food,' she says, 'a part was cleared. Most. You wouldn't know though, looking at a line of pines afar. What's so special about trees?'

'There's a rule,' I say. 'If there's more people than there's trees – the end has come.'

'It's often about space,' says Solène. 'But Jean-Luc says that all comes from heads that's packed to burst with brawn.'

'When it's done,' I say. 'After the end, the rest is stuff you wouldn't want to touch.'

'Money, slavery, whacking your neighbour if you can't love them,' she says. 'Or maybe they're unlovable.'

'We don't get far this way,' I say.

'Well,' she says, 'it's your business, if you want it complicated. Nothing's unexpected, but you don't need get used to anything that comes along.'

*

'I give up,' says Sami. 'I don't know what you want of me. Death – the best option... How'll you all honour me?'

'Well,' says Mélusine, 'we all, except Jean-Luc who did the test, all of us have Arab parents. So of course...

'A tribute,' says Solène. 'Trumpets, perhaps.'

'And did you love me?' Sami asks.

'You're gone,' I say. 'What we love of you is only in ourselves.'

'You, you bastard,' Sami says. 'You've got two wives, Lénick and now Solène. No one loves anyone round you. I have a finale. You'll have good riddance.'

'Bless you, Sami,' I say. 'Ask about some help for us down here.'

'A horse?' says Sami. 'Like in Puccini.'

'If we can't book Buffalo Bill, we'll get Abd al-Qadir, you bet,' Jean-Luc says. 'But not here on the stairs. The countryside!'

'I'm satisfied,' Sami says. 'I don't regret living, though I'd like to have seen the river just once more.'

'Oh, you'll see it!' says Solène. 'I've the obol ready too.'

'He's gone,' says Mélusine. 'That is – he hasn't. What'll we say he died of?'

'I'm not filling in forms about a corpse,' says Jean-Luc. 'If he's an illegal, not registered, we'll end up doing his sentence. In a month – he will be air. Wrap him, Mélusine – that's a Tabriz, full of holes...ideal! He'll slip through like a wear and tear.'

'I hope wherever he ends up,' says Mélusine, bundling him in the carpet. 'He doesn't come back. He did little while he was here, save change the scene, the music too – sometimes you could play it loud, at others, you could hum... If there's no change of scene, time's ended, and the villains are forever the same one. Ali – he might be a revenant, though most people seem to have his name, they can't all be the twelfth Imam. He was an innocent – I can't think innocence ends the world. He's not the one they're waiting for...'

'The end – it'll be one foot following the other,' Jean-Luc says. 'The whole cast tramping on. So much for philosophy!'

'Ali was merely good,' says Solène. 'Like Sami. They leave nothing, not even shades and shadows. My mother – she stole, created beauty and a refuge. I think – she was quite bad, all bad. This place is full of it, her act. Maybe another act – it could be mine. Everything else, all to come. Instead – she's reviled, and she's still all around. Ali, he was her friend, and they say friendship's good. I don't think it counts. Ali's forgotten, he won't come back, but no one says tut-tut...'

'Quiet, Solène!' says Mélusine, much agitated. 'We're all like that – thieves or moribund. There's no refuge, silly girl. That's my lesson – it's all gotten complicated, since you were born. Then, there were few sorts of people – rich, poor, and preachers. Now, there's a profusion. Listen! Learn! And deal with it!'

'You and Jean-Luc,' says Solène. 'You were tall poppies – Mélusine, you were a counsellor of state, you filled big empty ears: Jean-Luc brought philosophy to the TV. But now...'

'I know, Solène,' says Mélusine. 'Now, we have to fit Sami on the slow train's baggage rack. We need you to help lift. Guys like us – we're always laden down, our bundles of cheap stuff – in this case, wholly valueless. No one will question us, I hope. Our bundle's a cadaver nameless, not even Made in China.'

'I want things to be as they should be,' says Solène. 'And live as I should live.'

'Take this end, Solène,' says Mélusine. 'What we're doing is illegal, what we propose to do – don't ask. Look bold.'

'...and him, I can't stand him,' Solène says, pinching my arm, putting out her tongue at me. Winning at *bouchkazi*'s brought me no rewards...

★

At the station, we hoist Sami up, me and Jean-Luc, like we'd a carpet, hawking it around.

'Your uniform is lovely, Karlheinz,' shouts Mélusine. 'I'd take you for a lover – but I hate the intimacy, sooner or later I would need to eat you up...'

'Where's the enemy, Karlheinz?' Solène asks.

'We hope it's the Chinese,' he says. 'They negotiate, until you cross their line. The Russians and Americans – we don't have a chance. Heroism's our speciality – but there's more likely to be poor guys flitting in, for us to hassle and to herd... The waiting – it's the dullest part... We might form a band...'

'A gang?' I ask.

'Oh no,' he says. 'For music. When Vienna didn't fall, the Turkish bands roamed all around, in vogue for weddings, feasts, and all that stuff.'

'But inconclusive, Karlheinz,' Jean-Luc says. 'And then there's guys who bans the bands – the popes, the caliphs...'

Oh no – here's Lénick: she pinches me, and says, 'There's guys who'd ban the book my aunt, Gisèle, has kept. You –' and she pinches me, I've no defence for fear of dropping Sami – 'And your *bouchkazi*, nearly broke her book, her bank...'

'What's your instrument, Karlheinz?' asks Mélusine. 'We'll need a tune before we dump poor Sami here.'

'There's this large and sonorous drum,' he says. 'It's like the wheel of fortune. It's in tune with hearts – the sound goes through you like you were an empty room...'

It's true – this Turkish music rocks, and guys are running from their tents and foxholes – brass and wood all warming up...

'They get it off the gypsies,' Lénick says. 'How I'd love to run away with them – but they don't run, no more...'

'No, Lénick,' says Mélusine, 'they don't run, they're pushed. Don't let's fall in these cheap pleasantries. Music, ho! And then the dance, though it may seem inappropriate... Sami won't mind – it's quite his universe. And my big scene...'

'The scene is mine,' Solène says. 'I cared.'

'But I've the brighter voice,' says Mélusine. 'More noble birth. That's how it goes in culture – Sami knew...'

'No, Mélusine,' Jean-Luc says. 'This isn't archaeology – there's nothing hidden under stones, no sentiments, behaviours we might pretend to excavate. Nothing is stolen, nothing belongs. Everything is words, all is made of air and coloured in – the past: is no one's. If we forget – there is no penalty, no sign, we sing to make a noise, to show we're here and in transition, the sounds, they dissipate, the voices

... don't adhere to anything, the scores are soundless on a page, all is air, poor Mélusine.'

'Let's get it over with,' says Mélusine, annoyed.

'The best bits should be mine,' Solène says. 'And then we'll burn him, release him, up he'll go, a golden wood chip...'

'You'll burn down what fucking trees are left,' says Lénick, who's no part, no voice: 'Jean-Luc is right – Sami hears nothing, all the drama he's arranged – there's not a scar, a furrow drawn... He and the audiences – nothing, washed over by invisible waves that bear it all away – applause, the scenery that clatters in the dark... All left not clean, not barnacled, no limpets, no river weeds, nothing adheres...'

'That is our tribute, Sami,' I say. 'We've found the words... We float you, into your myth...'

'I've some business, guys,' says Mélusine ... off she runs. That mansion, Whistler – maybe beyond the line of pines... Oh, whistle!...

There is no whistle, just the soughing in the leaves, maybe beyond the crest, and running down, or rolling giddy, like the innocents do...'It's further than I thought,' she thinks.

'Why the Russians?' Jean-Luc asks Karlheinz, who says:

'Well, Vito tells us – they're better finding leaders, keeping poor smart people in a line. They have their own big place – they need to warm that, not build shacks everywhere, cover the world with ticky-tack... It's true, to make a change, they used the bullet and the jail more than some others – but it's normal up and down. And in and out:

Hey, Mélusine,' he shouts, as she comes sadly close. 'How did they dump you, when your advice turned out to be crap?'

'Oh,' says Mélusine. 'They didn't call, that's all. My counselling was good – they saw I thought them ignorant. That didn't sit. Subversive, that was me...'

'Exactly,' Karlheinz says. 'It's politics. Not policies: you dump the guy who disagrees with you, or maybe they'll compete. Americans – they have a hissy, go and bomb some distant guys ... the Russians, well, they pay you off or maybe you get infiltrated, reclaimed – the pay, says Vito, can be excellent. No strings, no rhetoric...'

'The trouble is,' says Jean-Luc. 'The Russians have no art. The Barge-Haulers – that just sums it up. The Chinese have ceramics – those will last. Those Russian poems – all on the one note. And as for novels – anyone does those, they're seasonal fruit. If you want monuments, Karlheinz – try Chinese ... and as for crispy duck...'

'Vito abhors a monument,' Karlheinz says. 'When he was into nursing, the suppression of the moribund – a holy exercise – no trace was left. Not of the patient, nor the agent. Cleanliness, not stones and pots that guys exhume and spin a story round... Perhaps the Chinese – they might do here... Best avoid people who resemble you, that's true. The Russians, though – they have the space.'

'Don't think of fighting anyone,' says Lénick. 'Complicity. Think cops, not suicide.'

Mélusine thinks, 'I could arrange Sami in the hanging garden – if only I could find it. If again they start to use it – he'd have company...' She doesn't speak. Sami's decomposing, silently.

'That carpet,' says Lénick. 'I've a use for that.' They unroll him. The carpet's hers!

'That's my robe!' says Solène. 'I wondered who'd got that!'

Sami's naked – that's the best, if you're a corpse.

'Suppose it's Arabs come?' I ask.

'We don't want that to happen all again,' says Lénick. 'All that history we've seen before. Everyone's mercenary, but those would want to tax us too...'

'Yes,' says Solène. 'We've been all that. Enough! The same history as everybody else but stretching out like gum...'

'Someone will come,' says Karlheinz. 'Whoever it is, they'll be like us.'

'I'll go look for a spot,' says Mélusine, and sidles off.

'It's like we're all on surf,' says Jean-Luc, straddling Sami. 'Each has a wave – some sink, some last until the end, are thrown and shattered on the sand...'

'I read that somewhere,' says Solène.

'I saw it yesterday,' Lénick says. 'I wonder why they keep repeating it? The best send-off – is Sufic yoga...' and she sets the carpet out.

'It's not authentic,' Karlheinz says.

'Look in a mirror, Karlheinz,' Lénick says. 'And see if any of yourself is visible. All or nothing is authentic – we established that. Except – perhaps, for you! You're not quite where or what you want to be. The yoga does you good – and naturally, what's true's repeated endlessly, it's boring, what do you expect?'

'Maybe I should have had my fling with Karlheinz,' thinks Mélusine. 'Most things are too late. I could have joined the masque, and been involved in carrying stuff...'

★

The rain comes down on Sami's corpse. Some take up their yogic attitudes – I copy what I can – it hurts. Then there's clouds – they race across the moon, the owls go 'oooo', the soldiers light their fires. A bugler tries his call – 'They call that "taps",' says Lénick. 'Who knows why?'

'It reminds the troops to take a shower,' says Jean-Luc. 'But – where's the body gone?'

It's washed away – perhaps another wave, hiding behind the last, has borne him all away...

'There is a rule,' Solène says. 'A body mustn't lie on stage. It makes vocal cords go slack, and so you cannot sing next day – Sami knew that...'

'The best way,' says Karlheinz. 'Is – bury yourself, dissolve. That way no one can falsify a body count. You're just not here, no longer on parade...' He weeps. He didn't much like Sami when he could.

'You are all dead, Karlheinz,' says Jean-Luc. 'You and all the soldiers. Waiting. For the metal globe, the wrecking ball, earth's twin – to drop. Waiting for the air, the tempest it will bring: what colour will it be, that kills you all? Maybe it will smell of night-stocks, or forget-me-nots... It will bring remembrance – maybe a romance ... a concert – wandering in the interval... talking about the orchestra, tipsy with the scent of someone you desire... Although – maybe I have the context wrong... You never went to concerts quite like that, finding a man, a woman, wanting to talk of time, quiet, maybe no word...'

'We're all dead,' says Karlheinz. 'We can do anything we like. Before our turn comes round, do anything: load tricky stuff in tubes and fire it off. Shells – from no sea – chocked full of air. The smell of cyclamens, a smell no one has ever lived through, never been described... What colour is that air? It blows, quite indiscriminate, breath from sick lungs, breathed over us... And will we see it first, the colour? Or after? It's not possible that it kills us colourless, banal.'

'Vedic air,' says Jean-Luc, knowingly. 'The oldest that there is. Those ice-cores – modern stuff! The air – who breathed it first? What animal, what proto-man? Every scent, all flowers and trees, and every fruit and herb... spark, tempest, clouds black and purple – all leave a trace on it, like bettle's paws, or fly crap on the glass...'

'This is it, then?' asks Solène. 'Sami's tribute, the great send-off? Your drowsy speculations?'

'A climax must be used quite sparingly,' Jean-Luc says. 'Or else you're always nearly getting there, and throwing them away...'

'Sami used to say that about Hindemith,' says Solène. 'They don't often do his operas, not even in Baghdad.'

'You're not in the right position to pass that kind of judgment, Solène,' Jean-Luc says. 'You need years of training before you can...'

'We're always training,' Karlheinz says. 'Until we wish that we were dead.'

'Weren't you a banker, Karlheinz?' asks Lénick. 'You must have trained for that?'

'Oh,' says Karlheinz. 'That was to be close to all the money. Then I was a fence. A spiv. A trafficker. You're even closer that way to the cash. They were wrong – money isn't excrement: it's skin. You cut it off people in oblongs. You wear it. When it's all over you – you are complete. That's why I joined up. Once you're in the bank – they always have a hold on you. Worse than the Jesuits. There's a step up: they said money stopped wars – now, yes, that is crap! We soldiers – when there's the catastrophe, we will be closer to the wealth that's left: building things up, saving guys who're stepping on the mines, mines of gold for us, worth the risk, a leg: safes – hanging off the walls and ripe...'

'I heard there's infiltration, Karlheinz,' I say.

'No one attacks these villages head on,' he says. 'There'd be a fight. There's nothing profitable here. There's many groups – they take the territory where no one lives. It's strategy – there's nothing there. Except faith – but who wants that if you don't have it first – it's not the rare stamp that fills the last gap in your page.'

'I don't see that,' Solène says. 'A faith's supposed to fill big gaps.'

'Gaps? What gaps? In what?' Karlheinz asks. 'Remember the kamikazes, remember those Jews in revolt, the caves: that would be altruism, I believe. Gaps? I don't follow you, Solène. The suicides weren't thinking of you, not at all. Altruism's about yourself.'

'I told you, Karlheinz,' Jean-Luc says. 'You argue like a pig. I can't get anywhere with you. We have to think – "what next".'

'Don't go in the trees,' says Karlheinz. 'Marauders are everywhere – the countryside is full of predators. Some parts – we've fenced, we tightened the food chain, there's culls and food for who are left, patrols, all that. Country reservations – like the Indians used to have, before they thought "casinos!" But if there's just the grass, the pines – keep off!'

'I think,' says Jean-Luc, 'soldiering is not for me. Nor this new nature that you've engineered. Philosophy's a dud! I may go into metaphor...'

'Oh yes!' says Lénick. 'Me too. But different, Jean-Luc. People don't do their poetry now, and they can't read. Games, Jean-Luc! Gossip! Snaps with my little Brownie! That squirrel on the fence! Like making quilts – or patching up old frocks, then all the patches make a new one – sheets and dusters, snot and sperm, and fur... There's cookies too...'

'That isn't me, Lénick,' says Jean-Luc. 'I fancy analysis ... how the world shapes, science, and all that. Gossip, Lénick, but higher up than yours.'

'It all sounds like parody,' I say. 'There's millions with that thought – and then... They're ruined, on the lam or on the pills and looking for a tent. No laws will help – so, you must work outside. Outside the laws. I shan't tell how...'

'Cheating escapees, you mean?' Solène says. 'Maybe I should be a spy, and sneak and tell on you...'

'They don't pay for that,' I say. 'That's being a volunteer.'

'That's what I am,' Solène says. 'I didn't ask for anything. Especially not for you.'

★

'Mélusine,' Karlheinz says. 'You wander off – you'll fall into a zone, a camp – a structure where they hold the escapees. It isn't you. I know how it was – when you were on the highest trees – the feeling grew – of nausea. The shaking, and the panic. That's evolution. Physiology. Vertigo. Mistrust, excess, of air. It's all ephemeral, that stuff: it's why Jean-Luc found his ancestors, and got his document. Between him and his forefathers, a nothing: a space, some methane – all in all, a void. Now, where you are, you'll stay, no running round. Things are resolved, dear Mélusine, they pass from life to paper, quicker than you can imagine. I'll show you what is permanent. My trade – that's permanent, it doesn't flit: banking and soldiery. That's what we're made for, Mélusine. We won't go back, not to the city, where you haven't paid the rent. Poor Jean-Luc, poor Lénick – a life of squeezing a false coinage, a nothing cash from air… Now, come with me, and see the countryside – it's dark but all is visible…'

They climb up on a knoll. 'Yes, yes,' says Mélusine. 'I've seen the little fires like that – in Chile, maybe, where the miners light a fire to warm them up before the undergound…'

'Oh, Mélusine,' Karlheinz laughs. 'They don't dig now, they scrape!'

He points – it's dark, you can see everywhere: 'That's us,' he says – a bunch of tents, dark limpets on black rocks. 'That's someone else,' and there's green humps, sea monster dwindling through the green. 'That's them' – there's round grey lumps, a porridge on the scree… 'It's stasis,' Karlheinz says. 'They'll throw a bomb or two, but all's decided somewhere else...'

'Oh?' asks Mélusine. 'And where...?'

'Of course,' says Karlheinz. 'You were into that, the give and take, rewards and punishments, the good, the bad. The thing to watch,' he says, 'is gas. Air's gas, of course – if you don't have it – maybe you're too high up – you're dead. I have in mind another peril. The gas that looks like air, but must be slightly lighter, slightly heavier, so that it drifts and mingles, hides, pounces on you... it's white and yellow, umber, black... There's Tantric colours, and the air is always changing, letting this monster live, that other gasp and terminate... The changes make you cough, or cry, or die. You need to have a colour sense, because of course, there's danger, it goes thick and thin – there's mostly air benevolent you see, the mist, the dusk, the seasons... But that's gloom! We could lie here, maybe concoct some love, dear Mélusine...'

'Oh no, Karlheinz, there's snakes', she says.

'Snakes don't know good from bad – they tempt, that's all. They suffer too – they all get killed at once, as people think that all are venomous,' he says. 'Now, I'm the tempter. I could tempt a snake – here's the good, and here's the bad ... both excellent to taste...'

'I think they know,' says Mélusine. 'Snakes, what's good and not, not just a tempt. Why bother with the prop, the snake? Besides, it's not about what's bad or not, it's all about you listening to the snake.'

'There's no ethic here,' says Karlheinz. 'It's what's good for you, or not so good.'

'Listen to me, then,' says Mélusine. 'I don't know good from bad – once, it was dig, and now it's scrape. You don't need go in the underground. Listen, Karlheinz... Silence. No snake. There, I'm not so bad, but not so good for you.'

'Oh, I shall listen, Mélusine,' says Karlheinz. 'There'll be other times – besides, we might lie here and – you can't hear the gas, or smell it till it's deep inside, and taken hold, and turned you into something else.'

'I might conceive,' says Mélusine, 'a child that lives in torment, choosing every day between what might be good, or probably is bad.'

'It's true,' he says. 'Mostly we spend our day like Lénick – in front of her, there is a – her – neutral brain, lit up. At least I have a gun. At times, I don't even need a brain, just a good aim. Solène has specialised in life and death. She's nothing else to do but wait. We stuck, now, all of us, in the village – we'll see each other every day.'

'Time to stretch my legs,' says Mélusine. 'Before we do something that changes the whole scene ... and you're to keep your watch...'

'Oh,' says Karlheinz, not disappointed that she's leaving. 'You hear the soldiers when they wake...there's trumpets... Now, Mélusine – don't go in the woods, it's not secured, there's people from all sides, there's buildings disused, used by who knows who ... we'll have to clear the zone... People disappear, they get absorbed, engulfed, sucked in, and others, well, like us, appear, though in the end there won't be anyone you'd recognise...'

'Silly boy!' says Mélusine. 'Of course I know all that. Today was not our day, that's all.'

★

Beyond the trees, there's scrub, black stumps of buildings, knocked and fallen down, and terra cotta bricks. There's no one hereabouts. No action, she's alone.

No Whistler.

She thinks –

'I thought the house was closer in.'

2

PEACE AND WAR

THERE'S A MAN on a horse – how tall they are, a step up for both species. He's not a jockey – they're full of excuses, always. He says, 'There's peace!'

'Can't be,' says the low-down guy. 'Aggression comes from self-defence. One leads to the other – they're a coin, reverse, obverse. Protecting peace – means preparing for the fight.'

'Don't be obtuse,' the mounted one replies. 'It's peace here, nowhere else.'

'That's a quarter horse you're on, so you need four to make a proper one, a team. And horsemen too. That's classical – the animals all interconnect, chained together ... the bees, the turtles, all in place, all eating one another, each essential to the plan, the great creation, born with its tail between sharp teeth, its own, or...' and the mournful small guy keens and rocks.

'I must be off,' the horseman says. 'Good news can't wait. The roads is bad – my steed might break a leg, like actors say. Good luck, sad sack,' and he whips his dobbin on...

*

'You should be like him,' says Lidia, dressed for hard work around the room. 'Maybe the good will turn out well for us – our relatives are all accounted for. We can enjoy what comes...'

'Well,' he says, Pavel, the pessimist, 'maybe it's best before they come, or when they've been... We should have a theory of all that. We don't live well here,' he persists. 'But down the road – we see the world's best magic city! There's the basilica ... every day they turn out a saint, something with wings, and talk of heaven, what's the best walk-up ... not to be gay, although that's what they mostly are – those frocks and carrying statues in the street.'

'You cut me out of that,' says Lidia. 'You came to Italy, because there's magic city there. And you were wrong – magic city's quite another place. Maybe it's heaven. Here for sure is not.'

'It's dark,' says Pavel. 'Time to be out. If the cops come...' He takes a trenching tool from behind – 'This bead curtain,' he says, 'it's from the Caribbean. Sucked candies. Sweet delights.'

'The cops won't come,' says Lidia. 'You should leave the tombs alone. That Etruscan stuff – they jail you if... That's probably the curse the dying guys put on it... You were in mind.'

'Black pots,' Pavel says. 'All the same. It's something material to be scared about. If there's prosperity – who knows what crap work we'll be made to do, to keep it floating up?'

'We're all punished, Pavel,' Lidia says, impatiently.

'I want it to be for something real,' says Pavel. 'Not statistics. Not unearthing – the dead, their useless stuff. Punished for what I am – that's why I wanted magic city, just down the road...'

It's true dark outside. There's stars – not seen for many years, or only in laboratories. 'So – it's not dark,' Pavel says: his mates go 'hush' in silence, 'There's stars,' whispers Pavel.

They tunnel at the bank. The cadavers have always disappeared. There's cremated bones, sometimes, like greyhounds' – they don't belong. Probably – a sacrifice.

'Death was more important to those guys,' says Pavel. 'Crushing.'

The chamber's empty – though there's a slab, two bunks... 'You don't often find them sitting round,' says Cristiano. 'Maybe they're visiting their neighbours.'

'Having a wedding,' Vito says. 'Ghosts. That's the best kind to pal up with. You should try for that, Pavel – marry that sour Lidia, before the Muslims start to screw her, then run, just like they'd do.'

Dishes for the hungry dead, empty. A smell?

Sour – unripe? A plum? Rotten. Sour milk.

'Oh, that's all disappeared,' says Pavel. 'It's like those figures in the shooting gallery – you knock them down, they slide off round the back, then up they come like new.'

'You, Pavel? Shooting?' Cristiano laughs.

'It's often hard not to do it, as it is to do,' Pavel says.

'I've found nothing,' Cristiano says, 'but I have the skill. I could dig the whole country up. Turn it over – pancake-like. What would it prove? That's there's nothing new? They pay you to do the archaeology – I know already what there is. I've been looking for it – but it's not a secret. You used to get paid for stuff – now, you go to jail.'

'Think of the cadavers,' Vito says. 'They need a lesson. They won't get eternal peace. That was the second choice – a scary trip, that was the first. Dead, you're bound to disappointment.'

'When I grow up,' Pavel says. 'Or when I've grown, and would have liked to be ... I've no idea. I'm like the dead, the absent dead – you can't tell what they did, or would have liked to do. That's me.'

'We'll kill your bottle, Pavel,' Cristiano says. 'New life! The grain that doesn't die!'

'It's all potatoes,' Vito says. 'They'd lie for ever in the ground – disturb them, and they blast your brains.'

I see Pavel, wandering to the house. 'No cash, Pavel,' I say. 'I haven't earned. No persecution, though.'

He says to fuck the cops, and hugs me, takes my cap and throws it in the air.

*

'Well?' Lidia asks. 'And did they fly at you, like owls or bats?'

'They'd had their visitors,' he says. 'You get what you believe in, Lidia. We shan't hear from them. No, nothing flew – maybe it wriggled past...'

'Find work, Pavel,' she shouts. 'Dig ditches! Or go croak in one.'

'That's snobbery,' he says. 'Everybody wants that kind of job – it is the best, the hardest one... You find all kinds of stuff.'

'If I was the heroine, I'd show you a terrible life,' says Lidia. 'The child.'

'It's dumped,' says Pavel. 'Using natural law – it isn't mine. Besides, you can't like everyone – especially if they just pop out from someone else.'

'You have to bring them into a belief,' says Lidia. 'I don't trust you with it – you change your mind... I took you in – I was sorry for you. Sorry for myself. We're all a clan, Pavel – people: the young's connected to the old, the good to the bad...'

'And yet there's tragedy,' Pavel says.

'That's the road I'm on,' says Lidia, like a stone.

'You work – you don't get paid,' Pavel insists. 'It solves the old-time problem – are you paid for your existence the next working day, or for today's last hour...'

'It's excuses,' Lidia says. 'Even if it's true.'

She drops a letter on the table. 'Look,' she says. 'For you. Deportation. They're good at writing letters, nothing else... See, that's you!'

'Send it back,' says Pavel. 'Write: Unknown. No One.'

'Then you're not who you say you are,' says Lidia.

'That sounds like hermeneutics,' Pavel says. 'The name – I remembered: the blinding light, on the Damascus road. It seemed quite apt.'

'You don't believe,' says Lidia. 'See where it's got you.'

'If you're a digger, you have to believe in it, religion. But not a word of it,' Pavel says.

★

'Ignore it,' Cristiano says: 'Come on the road with me. Here, you don't exist – and if you leave, you can't come back. Enjoy the paradoxes...'

'I have a surgery for waifs and strays,' says Vito. 'You're probably both of those. We tell you what the law is, can you be cured of it...'

'I'm not so sure,' Pavel says to both of them. 'It's peace. Everything will change.'

'They'll put you on a plane the same,' says Lidia. 'Send you somewhere, and your old neighbours – they will cut your throat.'

'I'll try another name,' says Pavel. 'Maybe you should too, dear Lidia, another life would suit...'

★

The next day – he's gone. Sometimes they let you stay in a place, but you must join their army. Pavel has short sight – he would only do in firing squads. Besides...

*

'I wasn't ready,' Lidia tells her friend. 'For a guy like him.'

'Well, there'll be other horsemen passing by,' her friend says, placating.

'Oh,' says Lidia. 'He wasn't one of those – his legs ... too short to straddle a big beast.'

'Maybe a hole fell in on him,' the friend says. 'His was a muddy life.'

'He wasn't really against women,' says Lidia.

'He's dead now,' says the friend. 'Bury him.'

'I want a place where everything is new,' says Lidia. 'Like the horsman promised. One world, and everything there is, it works, all for the first time, no plugging in, no little books that tell you what to do.'

'It's not like that at all,' the friend says. 'I read a piece – there's worlds that's gathered into groups, and thousands at a time, all organised – the higher numbers – the more complicated. It seems there is no end to them, you study, you forget, you purify, higher up you go, the less you carry, and your mind goes clean...'

'It's mathematics,' Lidia says. 'I was no good at that. It's true – my child – it was a burden to be dropped – but all the rest, this nothingness which is the end, and maybe it's transferred to something there that really is, and you aspire to be the mirror of all that... Means rolling bandages and hammering in those tent pegs, I presume...'

'No, Lidia,' says the friend. 'It isn't that at all. It is tranquillity. The others – they're all scattered on the path, there's space galore, just like when you look up – it may be sleeping on the floor down here, but twist your head –

there's nothing for a thousand years of weightless flight. No food, no booze – and all for free, you see the nothing stretching far above, and tiny lights, too small and wee for you to see – no matter, for there isn't anywhere to put your feet, no ground, nowhere to go...'

'It sounds quite terrifying,' Lidia says.

'It is,' the friend says, 'but what it is, must be.'

'Maybe it won't apply to us,' says Lidia, 'and maybe the horseman was mistaken. That peace – just relative. Either way, there's no compromise between what I want and what you know.'

'Think of Pavel,' says her friend, 'on the road, or buried in a cave. He'd not even see the paintings on the walls – Hell, mostly.'

'Your cosmology sounds more real,' says Lidia.

'And yours is more attractive, Lidia. But each of us is in the cage that doesn't suit,' her friend, Tracy, says.

'I feel so abstract with you, Tracy,' Lidia says. 'Maybe Pavel was an error... Spading up the dead...'

'Oh, you can't say that,' says Tracy. 'No one's an error – though some guys should be jailed. Yes – I'm feeling abstract, Lidia – we should go and find what is our time, what's new. Bangs, Lidia. Not earrings – a swag of hair, like mutton chops. Some women, they have jewels where you wouldn't think to look – that's quite excessive. Hair à la mode of Agrippina – we'll fit some on to you...!'

Lidia knows – there's her child – it will be there for years. Parked better than an automobile, but always – a twist. In the plot and banging on the door. And Pavel... silently he

leaves – what if he returns, sits in the armchair, never
talking of adventures, pits in his cheeks from all of them...?
You see him on the road – he's scared. What if he's hit with
sticks? Out there, the stars so far away, you're always
scared, your space so cramped, and anyone can take a shot,
piss on your fire or put your face in it. He wears a
Frenchman's hat, the kind with earflaps tied on top – not
the classy leather kind you used to find in Kiev – the cloth
sort, letting in the rain. Quite a dare for Lidia, letting him
in, then scratching and screeching till he goes – quite a let-
down for Pavel, his sound cosmology, kept to himself.

*

The joint says 'Beer and Love' – so of course, you go right
in. It's all a stereotype – it reassures, though, if you think,
quite bizarre. Pavel parks his sack, down by the rest.
They've put the TV on a loop – it keeps on shouting
'Goooooal', to keep the guys awake and pepped.

'What do you want, Pavel?' the barman asks. 'Think
carefully ... some don't.'

'A flat road,' Pavel says, 'slight incline downhill. No
horsemen, please...'

'Hmmm,' says the barman. 'Maybe you've been
coached. See – the mirror – it's important for us ... see if
your image moves while you stay still.'

It does: 'You're up there with the best,' the barman says.
'Now – see the Buddha at the shuffleboard? Mostly you see
him sleeping, reclining – eyes shut and meditating. This
one's a whizz! Darts too – a speciality.'

'I'll take off my hat,' says Pavel. 'And I'll challenge him. Tric-trac.'

'He'll win,' the barman says. 'You don't come in here often. Why don't you bring your lady?'

'Oh,' Pavel says. 'I mean harm to no one, but... Lidia has her world. She dresses up, when she is sad. She doesn't go for sport, being exhausted, blacking out, all that.'

'She has her world,' the barmen says. 'Don't you?'

'For sure,' says Pavel. 'It may sound solipsistic, but yes, I have my world, me alone, wall to wall, ceiling to the stars beneath my feet. The dead are gone, the living are outside – they run the stores and fight the wars – I see and hear it all, but I'm alone, eyes in a skin, and ears tacked on.'

'That's all of us,' the barman says. 'Now, sit down here beside these two – Tansy, Robbie. They're not into sports – they come here to get drunk. If they were sober, they'd see the kind of place it is ... and weep. You're used to grimy beerhalls, Pavel ... these two, they're a cut above.'

Tansy – how beautiful she is – not too tall or short, too hot or cold, and not too sober for a chat...

'That's a Scottish name,' says Pavel. 'You can see the rowan tree outside the house – the witch lives there, so's not to come indoors...'

'Maybe it was that once,' says Tansy, turning her bare white shoulders in the light, and pulling down her sweater's neck. 'Scottish and remote. But anyone can use it now.'

'I'm getting messages,' says Robbie, pulling on some yellow boots, paying his shout and limping to the door.

'He checks at home,' says Tansy. 'We're spied on by some feds. He looks for cover stories – he's quite thrilled if we make out, us two – it explains the arms he keeps. Jealousy, you see – but really, he's complacent.'

'He sounds quite absent,' Pavel says. Undecided, nonetheless he holds Tansy's knee and kisses her.

'Would you believe?' asks Tansy, snuggling down. 'The politics! We all have countries, but just choose a wrong allegiance ... the hunt is on!'

'This place,' Pavel says, 'is nothing special, but it oughtn't to be here.'

'I expect they found it in a book,' says Tansy. 'Once, the to and fro was camels. They carried fashion. Perhaps this place is where you'd want to be: beer and love. Who hasn't wanted that? Or did you think something exalted beckoned you? But have your game! He's waiting over there...'

'Is it a real buddha?' Pavel asks.

'You know that's a silly question, Pavel,' Tansy says.

The buddha sands the table. My! it's fast. The rocks streak up and down, red and green, like in the universe.

'Nothing sticks,' says Pavel. 'Off they fly. I'll never beat you, Buddha, you will never win.'

'Don't say stupidities,' the Buddha says. 'Enjoy yourself. Drink. Make love with Tansy – not in here, of course... Your life – everybody's life – is all about everything. It holds it all, all knowledge, every error. Concentrate!'

'I had bad times with Lidia,' Pavel says. 'And then there's Robbie too.'

'If you don't start to write the story, it'll never reach an end,' the Buddha says. 'There's danger all around – that's why I mostly sleep, recline and meditate. You'd not want crying all the time! Besides – there's fun in here, don't underestimate. These guys – they don't have cash for poison bombs.'

The board's now free – some guys start off – my! how it's slowed. No one wants to lay down sand. They heave the rocks, heavy now as sacks of lime.

Pavel and Tansy go outside: the sign says – like it used to: America Bar. It's late – that must be the band, guys straggling in. A singer in a country hat – she's brown, the union's blacked them all. There's no one left to hear.

'I'll have to clean you up,' says Tansy. When they're there, she runs a bath. 'If you take the Buddha seriously,' she says. 'Here's strawberry leaves – I'll float them, so's your bugs will find a raft. Your future's in the bedroom, Pavel...' and she minces out.

Pavel is clean.

On the bed there's Tansy, Robbie, naked and asleep. A screen beside them, lit – there's a spidery code: a plot, research, stuff secondhand, pricey, for sale...

Pavel puts on his dirty clothes, walks on.

*

'You're not afraid of me?' asks Mirko, broken down. 'I'm waiting for the fix, falling into step, a few metres, no more...'

'The people here,' Pavel says. 'It's fine they didn't go to school, but – they don't know anything. Not songs, not trees, not who the enemies are... And the priests – they read the mystic books, but they can't heal a wound or charm a fox...'

'You must come from far away,' says Mirko, ingratiating, not so subtly.

'I left my sack,' says Pavel, 'all my stuff – the dirty clothes, the mug.'

'Maybe the mug is you,' says Mirko.

'Well, there was a couple in the bar...'

'Oh, I imagine!' Mirko says. 'Gangs or terror, maybe for an orgy or a theft.'

'They washed me,' Pavel says. 'Though it may not seem like it.'

'Everybody here,' says Mirko, 'sees all the world, possesses what they see ... like you, like me. Each one, all different, the view depending totally on where you shift your eyes – but everything. All swept up, into the same dusty pile. All there, each scene and every content, every vase and every box...'

'I know,' says Pavel. 'I wonder though – would Tansy have been like Lidia? Was I just the same?'

'The problem's you,' says Mirko. 'People see you as an animal. You don't talk like them, and you're the butt. You're idle, and you smell. You don't worship, nor blaspheme. You tramp the road because that's what beasts do – your friends, who let you dig, they roam because they're paid to do it.'

'And yet here's many like me, like us,' Pavel says. 'There's peace, the horseman says, and so the roads are safe. But it's true – my friends – they were tormented.'

'Of course!' says Mirko. 'They're the last. After them – it's Golems. We don't believe in souls – it's not that they'll be soulless – nor that they will be expunged. They'll go on. Rare earths, Pavel – the best are made of those. The rest – well, any clay will do, or stone paste, kaolin. Those make the different kinds.'

'It sounds quite reactionary, that stuff,' says Pavel.

'It may be,' says Mirko. 'You can deny it, naturally. You'd not feel better for it. It's quite irrelevant, of course, trying to escape those consequences, to live by rules archaic – that's all gone by. Work – maybe you didn't want it, and in any case – it wasn't offered. Golems, Pavel... War and peace – up to them, out of our hands. They fly the planes, put out the flags. When you broke into those tombs – did you find life? Of course not. When it's gone – that's it. That's us. There's nothing vital lies between us humans and the creatures made of earth. Nothing that distinguishes – they're us, like we shall be, inert.'

'It sounds old movies,' Pavel says. 'They do it on TV to make flesh creep.'

'Those are our tales,' says Mirko. 'They're not true, and neither are they false.'

'Forgive me, Mirko,' Pavel says. 'To me you're full of kitsch at best, at worst – delusion, madness. You sit alone in your automobile, it turns your head. You're alone, but in the swim, the flood. You long for crowds, you're scared of being lost in them.'

'Good!' Mirko says. 'My automobile's repaired. I'll go my way, you yours. Without a tale, travel is meaningless. We'll see who reaches some destination – we'll never know who's right..If being right was in our heads...'

'It won't be me,' Pavel says. 'I've no hypothesis.'

Mirko drives off.

'He could have given me a ride,' thinks Pavel. 'All the clay I've dug... "Over that threshold I dare not step", the song says – fearful of the clay grown tall.'

★

It's night. Pavel's sitting on the kerb.

'You, who tread the road,' says Coralie, sitting beside him – 'I envy you. There's so much...'

'No,' says Pavel, 'we're husks. There's nothing, over and over, stories we remember from the city, and traduce.'

'My idea,' says Coralie, not listening, not caring, maybe – 'There's abandoned villages all around. We fix them up. Be interesting. I want new people, not Italians. Beurs. Not just from the Maghreb, but all kinds – even like you, who we don't know where you come from, or why, and where you'll end.'

'They say the Arabs didn't get this far,' says Pavel. 'But don't believe it. Etruscans and Arabs – maybe some Turks as well. They left their melancholy, and the longing for another country. Nothing more. That's Italians. Lots of things and nothing in particular.'

'I'll show you where we'll live,' says Coralie, maybe not understanding.

'We'd never fix these up,' says Pavel: the iron gate's been forced, the village street is dust, the houses piles of stones, quite unadorned, no doors or window frames, earth floors.

'Oh fiddle!' Coralie shouts out. 'You boys do wonders with your arms and legs. We'll sell some home-made drugs, have a parade – and every evening bring the goats to run the length – like there was marble. Then cuddle in our cots.'

'They took the windows and the floor, the doors, the tiles – dug up their dead, prised out the godhead from its niche – it's over, Coralie,' Pavel says. 'Leave it be.'

'You haven't understood, Pavel,' says Coralie. 'Look who's allied with who. The battles halfway won – the claims, the arms. And those ideas – a broth, or vanity. We need to find some piles of stones, rounded with departure, farewells, disuse for ever – maybe sown with salt. In such a place – we'll pass unseen, survive. Wars are the tide, Pavel – receding if you are not drowned. You choose the good side – be careful, but the option's yours. It may not win – besides, that first choice, that is forever yours. All the rest is someone else's. If the good guys win – they'll make careers from being bad. That's what peace gives, Pavel, the chance of working on the being bad.'

'That village,' Pavel says, 'there's nothing there to eat. It's cold.'

'Oh,' says Coralie, 'I've friends who understand all that – tents – large ones – made from webs and mist, the food you gather as it slithers past...'

'Why then,' Pavel asks, 'do I feel it's wrong? I've made the right decision all the time – Livia, Tansy, pacing down the road and sitting here... And yet. It's wrong, I feel it's wrong...'

'To answer that,' says Coralie, 'you need philosophy. I don't know a philosopher who'd want to come along... Let's try that bar – see how it jumps!'

'I...' Pavel starts to say.

'No, not a word,' says Coralie. 'Have you carved one, written one? Said one that two people can remember? A word? No! You're like the rest. Nothing said, nothing remains, nothing remembered. There's things that people know, they may not see, may never happen – but they know. Like Palestine – the guys that lose the wars, over and again – they know that in the end, they'll win, and it will be decisive. Same for the other side – they know they'll win and win – and lose. So it is with us – Pavel, you're a free agent, rolling down the slope. And yet you know one day you'll stand, run, and...'

'Yes, I know,' says Pavel. 'Let's not spell it out. But – if the next explosion's big like you say it is – knowing about the future's quite irrelevant.'

'Oh Pavel,' Coralie says, 'don't think banal. Those women, dull, your travels one drab happenstance treading on its brother's heels. Try to rise above yourself, be worthy of the other "you" you'll be...' and she's in the bar, looking for philosophers, and for someone who'll find food where no one would like to look...

'Fear and intuition,' Pavel says. 'That, you offer. But those are always with me on the road.'

'You can't have enough of them,' says Coralie. 'They're reasonable and true, the two of them. Guys steal your sack, hit you with their sticks – and you mistrust all the other guys who've taken to the road. You're not mistaken, not at all.'

The bar is full, the band plays 'Caldonia', very hot and strong – everyone is drinking fast, but nobody seems drunk. It's the place they've all been dreaming of.

'Your friends,' says Coralie, 'they'd like to come with us. Cristiano, Vito...'

'Forget the "us" for now,' says Pavel. 'Vito's a lawyer who likes to break the law. Cristiano's on the road, but always wins the argument and finds some work. It's like they say – "the devil finds work for evil hands to do..."'

'That's new to me,' says Coralie, quite fascinated. 'You've known crap people, Pavel. They'll have tainted you – it doesn't matter. To survive, you don't need be good, believe in states, in socialism, or why your country disappeared. Or anything at all – just – you need be sitting tight, in the right place.'

'If there's no right place, Coralie – and you've chosen a nameless one – there's walking,' Pavel says. 'A heap of walking – ask the Armenians, Syrians – now, that's walking!'

'My parents were survivors,' Coralie says. 'You judge the situation, so you master it. Your friends dump you, you drop your friends...'

This bar – is bright. There's no TV, the guys take off their overcoats to sit, some stand their boots beside the table. There's many philosophers, keeping mum – you tell them from the way they order so polite...

'While you were tramping round, Pavel,' says Coralie, holding his arm quite tight, ordering a jug with chasers – boiled eggs and horsecocks too. 'Things changed here. When you left – it was all laws, careers, and deference. You and your pals, for transgression and some cash must go out in the dark and nudge the long long dead. Now – there's no schools and hospitals. There's healers, but when your time comes round, you die. What did you expect? You don't need schools to get a job, to fix a roof, castrate a pig. The booze is made out in the back. There is the code, for punishments, vendettas – there's guys with memories so calibrated – nothing escapes. No kings and gods, no heroes, like in the song. Who needs those?'

'They all seem happy here,' says Pavel. 'No one's in uniform...'

'Oh fuck all that, the happiness,' shouts Coralie. 'That's nowhere written down. They trudge along, like they have always done – the only thing is: don't have kids. That way you won't have warriors, won't pollute the stream, frighten the eagles ... no screaming face toying with its food...'

'But us here,' says Pavel, attracted and bemused, 'We – they – don't seem old.'

'Oh Pavel! – there's exceptions, naturally. We sit here with our happiness in mugs and jugs – and who knows if there's copulations in the fields? The way home's dark and jiggledy – this, you understand, this is the natural life. The law, the word – expensive, murderous... Worn out,' says Coralie.

'Suppose it doesn't work,' says Pavel. 'It seems some guys elsewhere have kept their rockets and their gas...'

'That's why we need to find someone who'll do philosophy,' she says. 'This table full of drink – this is our trap for sages.'

'There's no soldiers here,' says Pavel. 'So – if there is a war, we all surrender. Occupation. No one gets hurt. But – what if they take the guys away, put them in mines, behind the tills and such...? The horseman said there would be peace...'

'That's what he meant – what you've just said. Maybe it's banal, a caricature. But – look around, Pavel,' says Coralie. 'These guys – they are not made for that, for doing modest slaving work and taking loans. But – you're right. Best be prepared. We'll hunker down, anonymous, unfindable...'

'For me, there's always been this goal...' Pavel says.

'Those that tried to hide themselves – some were the rich. Some died, unburied ... and invisible,' says Coralie. 'Some were celebrities. Who cares?'

'That guy,' says Pavel. 'Scrutinising us. He could have done philosophy...'

'He'll do,' says Coralie, beckoning. 'The gender doesn't count in brains, philosophy's not sexed. And you, Pavel – these little legs – the road has strengthened, lengthened ... you could be my horse ... your wizened stubbly face, screwed up like somebody's first draft – you could even be a horseman, one of them, the four...'

'A centaur?' Pavel asks. 'That, I could enjoy. Everything is backward here. A hybrid seems quite usual: before, women were the centre of the life ... here, the guys, they look like trappers.'

'I'm a trapper too,' says Coralie. 'Don't try to grasp these complicated things – at least in this beer hall – no one's insulting you.'

'And I'm the woman you've been looking for,' says the philosopher. 'Julia. I'll do brains and food – one feeds into t'other. I'll be two expert witnesses, brain and stomach, and follow you, right to the end – those horsemen galloping! – my hearing's well attuned to sounds of hooves...'

'You're the right sort,' says Coralie. 'I guess you'll study us, and we shall study you. Now, what we need's a guy to hoe and bait, then we'll be off!'

'This guy here?' asks Julia, pulling Pavel forward by her thumb, in his lapel. 'What's wrong with him?'

'He's to be strengthened up,' says Coralie.

'You are what you drink,' says Julia, chasing two shells of ale with something blue and swift. 'My thesis is – you think, what you have ate.'

'I read that somewhere,' says Coralie, unimpressed.

'Oh, I give interviews,' says Julia. 'Lots. The idea is this – your ganglia sit upon the rock, your knobbly cranium, waving their pinkish arms – nothing to do but wait for food. On the reef they sit, silent, patient. They die, of course – and that's your coral scurf, Coralie, the rock on which we build. What is dead – that is our knowledge.' And she laughs. 'You see that waiter, hiding by the pillar? He drinks your beer, then fills the glass with pee. That's what he thinks of you. You won't find out, complain, because you're poor and insignificant. You don't suspect – that's why you go on being poor. But here – Pavel is right – it isn't Italy, nor Europe, any more. "Beer and love", "America Bar" – we eat their food, we think like them. America. It's called the Genghiz Khan syndrome: they long to conquer and enslave, and then chill out. But – their food spreads everywhere, and then, through commerce, ours goes back to them, and so it's circular – they give us awful waffles, that syrup coaxed from plants – and they get back our crispy duck, *pirozhky, nasi goreng...* World food, Coralie! It's conquest! With a cuisine for omnivores, we could think everything. Instead, those poor anenomes, our ganglia insist – we think of food.'

'There may be none where we are heading,' Pavel says.

'Then we won't think of anything at all,' says Julia. 'You may feel hungry – but a feeling isn't scientific. Not susceptible to reasoning... Not communicable, and not described – pleasure and pain, so close; vengeance and repentance, guilt and justification...'

'You're very flexible,' says Coralie, disbelieving.

'That's what brains are for,' says Julia. 'Americans! They need to have us eat their food. They want to see the slaves lined up and shackled in their fast food joints ... waiters, chefs ... slavery, Coralie. Those food stores... That smell of ratty biscuits and the pisslike oil...!'

'And that's philosophy?' Pavel asks. 'Does that account for all the talk of language, ethics and the universe, those equations and imperatives?'

'Yes,' says Julia. 'What did you expect? That's what there is, and all the rest is poetry that sneaks by since it doesn't rhyme.'

'Your argument,' says Coralie, 'is flawed. Everybody eats world food – conquest is in the brain of everyone. It's toxic – eating's what we die of – you do it all your life, it does no good, and in the end, you can't. It's like those guys who ate cadaver brains, and got the sickness, not the strength... And, now, just to survive, you must impoverish the rest... Your every meal means other guys will starve.'

'I hadn't thought of that,' says Julia. 'Maybe I should eat more falafel and manioc, broaden my mind... Coralie, you're a genius – you should publish: diets and recipes...'

'Coralie,' says Pavel, 'you are my soulmate, that's for sure – but you two parrots, Julia and you, squawking this banal stuff – I can't trip with you...'

'Then Julia is right,' says Coralie. 'You shall eat beans, and not join in the cultivated discourse woven by us above. Instead, you'll hoe the pulses.'

'Coralie,' says Pavel, 'I don't think Julia is suitable – the hardship, isolation that we face... To her, oil and beer are urine. To me, they're precious, colours don't enter in...'

'Ideas,' says Julia, 'they go in and out. Round and round. We stand behind the pillar... Sometimes we despise the clients, sometimes we're thirsty – nothing to be done. When it goes in...'

'That's philosophy,' says Coralie. 'You must admit, Pavel.'

'Someone must fix the village,' Julia says. 'Call a friend, Pavel.'

'Cistiano – he would come. You pay him, he won't stay.'

'He's your friend, Pavel,' says Coralie. 'He'll come, get paid. My friends don't stick. People think I'm quite a shit.'

'People are always right in what they say, Coralie,' says Pavel. 'But what of that?'

★

The offer's good – Cristiano comes. On the way, he's beaten, bad. It goes that way, especially if you carry cash.

'If you die, Cristiano,' Pavel says, 'Vito'll come to help. We'll find who did you in...'

'That isn't what a lawyer does,' says Cristiano. 'But, since you're not from here, Pavel, you're the prime suspect. When they accuse you...'

'We're friends, Cristiano,' Pavel says. 'We dug together.'

'It's family that counts, Pavel,' says Cristiano. 'And they tell us we've a family waiting for us when we croak.' He waits, patient, for his second birth.

'Suit yourself, dear Cristiano,' Pavel says. 'You've missed the chance for some last words – we could have exchanged cosmologies...'

'Mine's been set out in print,' says Cristiano. 'Yours – I shouldn't need to look at it.'

'Remember how we dug together,' Pavel says, trying to start a tear, a laugh. 'Those owls – breaking out the cave, and down we tumbled in the road with fright...'

'Empty tombs, Pavel,' Cristiano groans. 'Left unoccupied, the people resurrected, robbed centuries ago... We never found a full one. Empty tombs, Pavel...'

'And Lidia?' Pavel asks. 'Am I remembered there? A mismatch guarantees an easy victory for one of you – and did she realise she'd a deliverance...?'

'It's me that's dying, Pavel,' Cristiano says. 'Don't seize the thread that leads you back to where you start – that's what I'd do, except I'm keen to see what's next...'

★

'What shall we do with him?' asks Coralie. 'We learned nothing from him. What could we expect? We aren't responsible: those who beat him – they're just irresponsible.'

'He must be disposed of,' Pavel says. 'We can't leave him out the back. The authorities – know what is known. We're in the clear. We don't know anything.'

'An Etruscan burial, then?' asks Coralie.

'That was boys' games,' Pavel says. 'He'd hate those black plates and bottles, the earthy smell, the lamp gone out … no one comes, until the robbers do, by then the bones have gone – "death who steals everything, can't steal those mugs and jugs".'

'I didn't know him,' Coralie says.

'It makes no difference at all,' says Pavel. 'We'll take him to the village, leave him for the beasts, the wild ones…'

'There's no wild beasts left,' says Coralie.

'I can't think about it any more,' says Pavel. 'We all had families and radical ideas. Then we had Lidia, and walking on the road. What happens to Cristiano – every step makes it matter somewhat less.'

'We'll leave him out the back,' says Coralie.

'We'll need a still,' says Julia: 'I'll steal the coil, the rest we'll improvise.'

'I've always wanted houses – now I'll have a hundred. Pavel will fix them while we await the bang,' says Coralie.

'No, no,' says Pavel. 'That's a sickness. Accumulate, collect, until there is a crisis, then we fix it, go on to the next: it's madness. We patch the ruin, then conserve, collect some more – and then it's colonies on roaming rocks, and maybe stars – the pioneers set off in caravels and balsa rafts – and here we are, starfall, or planet ho! – exterminate the aliens and populate the universe. It's not survival, Coralie – it's hoarding. Unhappy here on earth? – another family, another life await, with all abundance that you couldn't get back here... It's like the bible – a few rules? No, stick it all in, invent and fantasise, we'll print the different versions, who cares, no one will read it anyway – it's like the writers ... the characters come round like in the shooting booth, that Dickens! – the same characters in different outfits, even collecting families... The painters – paint, paint paint, the dawn the midday and the dusk, the red the green the black, the smear the spot the stain... The poor guys making children – every shot's maybe a son, and if not, there's a daughter with a dowry that will ruin you, and all those sons – there's only one to get the single cow, the rest are poor and quarrelsome ... and if you've fortunes, they're so big they can't be spent, they're there for squandering and putting fortunes on a horse, a dream – it's madness, sickness, Coralie.

'We'll live, the three of us, in the one room, a plastic sheet to keep the snow away, and for a trip we'll find some magic fungus, for the rest we'll hunt and gather...'

'We can't do that, you idiot,' says Coralie, much put out. 'We cannot hunt, the area's reserved.'

'Alas, Pavel,' says Julia. 'I thought you were a modern type – instead, you're *facho*. I'd show you how to live a modern life – instead, you're a reactionary, you trudge the roads, you're ignorant and flighty, cruel, insensitive, unable to make friends, to have relationships, to join the swish and swirl of genius, invention...'

'We're going to the village to survive,' says Coralie. 'We're sane. We'll wait. I'm sure your life is your most precious thing, Pavel.'

'That's true,' says Pavel. 'Let's stow poor Cristiano, forget who did him in – the customary unknowns – up to the village, Julia... We'll have time to watch the sun set, sit on the stoup, and make our tale of it.'

*

Cristiano's waiting, in the outbuildings. Let him wait. The three survivors, go to the village, start to survive. It doesn't work. Each has a house, not fixed. It doesn't work out like it should – but it's not bad.

'I can't sleep with other people in the room,' says Julia.

'It's too intimate, then,' says Coralie, 'Leaving just me and him.'

There's no food – but there's a guy who visits with a mobile store. Julia has cash. 'I bet he'd sell us drugs,' she says.

They watch the frogs. A big one – they taste his skin, but don't hallucinate. There's fungus on a log – the frog, he tastes it – he hallucinates, they follow his example.

The guy who drives the van – doesn't sell drugs, but does take bets.

'If you double up, and do accumulators,' the guy tells Pavel, 'in a while, you'll win all the money in the world. And if they print some more, truckloads – then bet with gold and diamonds, then with chairs and spoons. Persevere, and win. Everything will end up here. The races won't be fixed – there'll be a pile of stuff, a mountain, Ossa on Ararat ... the cold and destitute, who've lost their skins, will see it from far off.'

Pavel tells Coralie, 'No more bets. What next?'

'There's love. Highly commended. Mowing the grass that's nearly tall enough to hide us all.'

'Grass or love?' says Pavel. 'Love is a feeling. You can't talk about it.'

'Yes you can,' says Coralie. 'Julia talks about it – her and me, our feeling – non-stop. It's conclusions you can't reach. And then – the money for the food is hers... There's children too, Pavel – they take up your time. And if they don't, there's cops and ambulances to bring them back...'

'Children is out,' says Pavel. 'It destroys our purpose. And if I scythe the grass – there'll be the refugees that want to come and stay – they'll see the houses... Then there's speculators...'

'You could collect some animals,' says Coralie. 'People do. They pet them. They look after them, have nothing in return – it's another of our fetishes, Pavel. We live by them. We're like bower birds – except they build their palaces to get some sex... We do it to scratch our itch.'

'That takes our mystery away,' says Pavel. 'There is no mystery, just building up. Coralie – don't mystify us three. We're sane and healthy, we have no affliction. We're waiting for the war that we'll survive. This time it'll be us in ceremonies – when all is done, the bad guys finished off, we'll have parades, remembering the dead, although we don't... Cops, soldiers, bands and priests...'

'There are bad guys,' says Coralie. 'Don't forget. It might be us. Though – I wonder how they do their ceremonies. Their trophies... Don't underestimate them, Pavel. Think of poor Cristiano – that was a massacre – and Vito thinks you had a hand in it – your invite to Cristiano, then no security: all that.'

⋆

'While we are waiting here,' says Julia, 'Pavel could hide away the stuff that should survive. The greatest, highest things...'

'There's stones here that abound,' says Coralie. 'He could carve them into semblances.'

'Stone faces. And call it Buster Keaton gardens,' Pavel says, taken with the thought: 'The boater, though...'

'That's easy,' Julia says. 'Mixed media. We'll ask the vanman for a stock...'

Each face takes a week. Multiples: who remembers those? They're not 'pretty maids all in a row' – but there's a marketable supply ... you'd need a gallery, an agent, a Vollard ... the vanman won't take some as currency, too heavy for his springs.

'There's wars all round,' says Coralie. 'But little ones. It's boring here.'

⋆

'You have talent, Pavel,' Julia says. 'You must do the three of us in stone. No fluttering things to intercede, no angel wings, no victories decapitated, defeats, no Lidia, no Tracy, no devils, and no Vito – all those guys you met along the road, Pavel. We – survivors – we're more important than the heads on Rushmore, or on dollar bills...'

'Who'd come to see us?' asks Coralie.

'Oh, there's evolution. Some beast, exploring, when we're gone. Something enormous, if it's superhot. Teeth like machetes, in three rows. A tail. Or slimy, buglike if it's cold or underwater. But intelligent – wow! They wouldn't need to read the books – they would intuit. Like we see two trees – they'd calculate the distances between a million things they cannot see,' says Julia, and weeps, maybe it's bathos, or she regrets ... her incompleteness.

She's a sport, abandoned somewhere on the noble path that leads up to perfection, glimpsing, then one day being – she hopes – the eye itself, with blue above... Oh Julia! – the higher up you go, the less you see. Here from earth, the sky – it should be black, it's not, it's blue: up there, the eye all-seeing, now just a patch of blue in blue, a blind spot, perfect though, a cerulean wall-eye ... the high point in the dome, the opening in the mosque, the crack, the breach, an eye that should be open to the eyes; though surely dead-eye could see through terra cotta, the clay that's sculpted cannily and quick, and goes to swarm alive about the rocks and acids in the universe...

'Yes,' Pavel says. 'My own face – it has a vegetable trend – not quite potatoes, more the rutabaga, but...' Coralie interrupts, 'Don't lament, Pavel. Shave off a millimetre – off my nose. And capture my mysterious grin … and clothes. Gingham? Silk? Or maybe we're all naked – entwined like snakes that know already what is on the tree, and good and evil nice and clear defined…'

'Oh Pavel,' Julia says. 'I know you think I'm frumpish, too much body hair. Make me a slick imposing kind: this is for eternity, remember. A touch of Jupiter about my lips, a trace of Nero on my brow, but breasts like pointy quinces – even, if you like a tease, like aubergines…'

'It's true,' says Pavel. 'Get things right. But you must help – quinces and aubergines are not the same. Maybe because you're hungry, had a fancy … even so…! We must be accurate, entire – every scar and piercing, blur and blot – they must be chiselled on. It has to be the whole of us, or else whoever comes after a billion years might think our bodies are like caterpillars'…'

The three stone figures, unrecognisable – not that you'd recognise the three if you see them in the flesh – are stood up in the grass. It's time to go. The statues – they will do.

★

'Wait!' shouts Coralie. 'It all makes sense. But – it's a paradox. We're the three survivors – but we'll die!'

'What did you expect, dear Coralie?' asks Julia.

'Don't you have a theory, Julia?' Pavel asks. 'About the thought, arisen from the food.'

'Oh yes,' says Julia. 'That's proven to my satisfaction. It's trivial. What do you want? – statistics, pills?'

'Then, say we go back to the bar – and find it isn't there,' Pavel insists. 'That stuff American – it's mostly disappeared, or dwindled down, years back...'

It's true. The bar has gone, a desolation stays.

'We threw it all away,' says Coralie. 'Our plan. Although I've seen the idea so many times ... the flight that's not imposed. It's rare. You run because your situation is not yours, it's unchangeable, and falling on your head. But – going back where we began, without illusions – we're just as impotent. We don't like what will happen to us, but we're bored when we escape.'

'You bastards took my cash,' says Julia. 'Your crap idea, Coralie...'

'You could have fed us with your thoughts,' says Coralie. 'Besides – there was the grass, songs of the frogs, the stars...'

'No enterprise of yours, all that,' shouts Julia.

'It finished when we put ourselves in stone,' says Pavel. 'That's how you know a civilisation's at an end...'

'You wait, Pavel,' shouts Julia again. 'The cops'll tax you with your battered friend... Ours wasn't even an experiment – we got our food off that guy, his van...'

'It's history,' says Pavel. 'First you avoid the wars – you massacre the indigenes, and send your troops to fight abroad. When this won't work – then, comes the fear. That's what it means, 'America Bar'. Bar None, the brand. You brand it on lost cows, it's the default. What I feel about the rest, the nations, all their crews – it's based on fact, my own experience, not prejudice, not envy, it's the winning recipe. I love everybody, one by one, of course. I garden,

Coralie, when I've a plot of land... Hearts-ease, to smother down the fear. The lager of forgetfulness, dear Julia...'

'You haven't got a clue, Pavel,' says Coralie. 'My revelation's this – you don't escape the way things are by going into nature...'

'That's where we are, we always are,' says Julia, much annoyed. 'There is no in and out. There's contentment, and there's not – that's all, they say.'

'You're bourgeois, Julia,' says Coralie. 'Adventure's over for your lot. Your class was stable like the spinning top, the tightrope guy, stuck in the middle, terrified, the wobbling pole...'

'You two are lost,' Pavel says.

'Pavel, you're just like all the other poor guys on the road,' says Julia. 'Pasty, wrong religion, no ideas.'

'No,' says Pavel, 'I'm special. I'm a winning combination.'

'You're a deserter,' Julia says. 'People want to make something of you.'

'No,' says Pavel. 'I didn't desert, I joined: people on the road.'

'That's not desertion,' Julia says. 'That's making a turn. Joining in. Desertion means out! You're not interesting, Pavel, not like me or Coralie.'

'There's few of us deserters,' Pavel says. 'We're poor and homeless. Then – we're invisible. My desertion's over – now I'll think of something interesting.'

'Black, woman, *facho*, deserter – there's no second chapter to all that,' says Julia. 'It's not like "child", "imagined", "kind". Those you can develop. There's no battle ever fought between deserters, no charity box, no medal, no shrine, no patron – nothing. No good or bad, good guys or bad guys – it's a cop-out. Flashes and bangs, epiphanies – old stuff: they happen all the time, to everyone... Maybe you had a scheme? Said it was a miracle...? Say something, Pavel. You can't! Desertion's mute.'

'True, I did leave,' says Pavel. 'A revelation. Not the army. Not me. Not exactly. I had illumination. The flash, epiphany – they say it changes your beliefs. If you start without them, they don't change – they're not your butterflies.'

'Oh come, Pavel,' says Julia, 'Everyone has had their communist friends ... belief that comes, then goes. Maybe you're ill and losing thrust, badly ill, if not today, then for what's to come.'

'Like all those Poles, who live in Jews' houses? They're dying off, but none of them was ill. Freedom, "Solidarity" – a bit rich, don't you think?' says Pavel.

'Oh snooty!' says Julia, exasperated. 'You're flat, Pavel – it doesn't mean the earth's that way. It spins, and so you need to cling or you're off into nothingness. Look at me – how I create, imagine... Poor Coralie – she doesn't have the brains, and so she needs to be the centre of herself. And no one cares, and no one sees.'

★

'You're the keeper of the castle, Pavel. The counsellor, the gatekeeper, chancellor, butler, majordomo – you see it all,' says Coralie. 'You'll wait your chance... Wait for the infant, the mad king – the soppy queen – then you'll be acclaimed, dear Pavel, you'll be the half-cock come to rule the roost. You even have the scandal – everyone that's big needs that... Cristiano, his body disappeared, and you the suspect. Ready for the final showdown, the duel on the precipice, Vito with his loaded dossier – yes, Pavel, you could be the hero of our time, the disenchanted leading the purblind, muttering against you, they'll trudge a continent. Something, Pavel, that's what you're looking for – you won't find it on your telephone, even if you search it all the day...'

'Yes, Coralie,' says Pavel. 'No doubt it's true, all that you say – it's just ... I don't want it, none of it.'

'You can't leech on to me,' says Coralie. 'It's Julia has the cash. She sold her thought – where did it go? Into the pile ... the autumn leaves, like the song says, Pavel. But she got royalties – round golden ones, stamped with a severed head.'

'Coralie,' Pavel says. 'You cast me as the smart servant, who stands behind some idiot's throne, not so smart I couldn't think to sit on it myself.'

'That's right,' says Coralie. 'You're not that smart, and not that bold. You got sucked in, and then spat out. It wasn't supreme destiny – just you.'

'That horseman – taking the wrong path – there's no guidance once you're on them,' Pavel says. 'Horses. It's this goddam peace. I can't remember when they didn't want to put me into uniform and hang a gun on me, or when some guy wasn't trying to take me out – and everybody else, – and seize the food, pee in the water, sing along that strummy hit with Beethoven. Now – peace: what do you do in it? All your relatives alive and breeding, your friends around you all your lives, nothing ending, on and on, everything promiscuous, proliferating... And thrones and majordomos – they give the orders like before.'

★

'We could tell Vito how Pavel did the killing, hid the body,' Coralie tells Julia. 'That would teach them both! Cure Pavel of his misogyny ... you don't have to be a genius to spot it – it clings to them like acid scurf on pipes. And Vito – can persecute the innocent! Pavel says how in some countries, women do everything, and the men, they drink and fight, like on the savannah. Ride their horses, too.'

'Well, Coralie,' Julia says, nonplussed. 'I like drinking and fighting, just as much. Why not, though? These legal things go on for ever without end, it means you have long life. And if you've cash, you live until it's gone.'

'I want Pavel to tell the truth,' says Coralie.

'You're too provocative, my dear,' says Julia. 'We know the truth – because we made it up ourselves.'

'He knows something more profound than what we got from living poor,' says Coralie. 'This peace – it's short sentences. Sure, those exist, but not forgiveness, not at any price.'

'Pavel believes he's expiated whatever he had done before. His wandering, robbing only from the dead... That is the best we all can do. It's quite conclusive, Coralie. Don't try to add a mystic twist,' says Julia.

'Crusoe had peace,' says Coralie. 'But wasn't happy. He wanted off, he couldn't stand the peace. His only wish – back to the empire, on the men o' war.'

'Crusoe deserted,' Julia says. 'He had no choice – alas, he took his culture when he fled.'

'He was the lookout, or at the helm. He survived because he saw the rocks,' says Coralie. 'Then wished he hadn't. So he said.'

'He was lonely, because he was right,' says Julia. 'He saw enough to save himself. This was his place he'd found – a desolation, bursting with abundance. He couldn't live it through. The bible – gave him that unwanted boss, silent, vindictive: company. He managed all alone. He should have killed the black. He wanted his other self, the dark savage – a mistake. A weakness. It didn't help him get off sooner, and meanwhile, he'd fallen in the slavery trap. He was lucky there was no woman, or out would come misogyny, for sure.'

They're clever, Julia, Coralie, and so they hug.

'The castle,' Pavel says. 'You see them all around – the towers. They're refuges, of course – there is no sally-port. You have slow elevators – you're trapped up in the crows' nests. So, they're for permanence. They're built for peace eternal, for defence.'

'This tower is tall enough,' says Julia squinting up towards the sun. 'We'll take the top floor. There's big and little guys all over – it's feudalism: – no special end, no responsibility. Loyalty's enough. Nod to the chief – do what you want and pay the rent.'

'No,' says Coralie. 'If we are Crusoe – nature must be against us. Accountancy as well. And we three aren't serfs, we're motivated – not by cash or property, but life.'

'Oh how pretentious!' Julia says. 'You won't find better castles – no one attacks this, it's too tall.'

'Crusoe!' shouts Coralie. 'Peace and survival – remember that...!'

'They'll find you, Pavel,' Julia shouts back. 'Even if you're framed – they'll walk right in. You'll have to tell them everything, and maybe you'll get off. Or maybe you will take the rap for all the rest...'

'Crusoe had resources,' Julia says. 'And we know – he knows – it can't end in silence, he'll return and tell the story, his version of himself... It would be better if Friday made a stand, exacted justice – and brought the white polished sailor's skull to show. Maybe he should have eaten him, and crunched his bones, the rowdy Robinson, the bigot...'

'We have to leave Pavel here, alone,' says Coralie. 'Here in the suite... The cops will come for what he's innocent of doing, and he'll know what he did – the Damascus road – that no one tells, and maybe he's forgotten. No black will come up here, and we two, Julia – we'll go down, sit in the bar... He left all the others – everyone. On every side, the good and bad, Pavel left them all to die.'

'That's surely part of it,' says Julia. 'But he's much attached to life. Like them.'

'Leave him here, up in the clouds, no power, no booze, he'll see the day turn into night, and back into the light, and on and on, no respite and no rationale... Except the world is round and swings suspended on a string we cannot see, nor touch or cut...' says Coralie.

Pavel sits hunkered on the grey moquette: 'Off you go,' he says. 'I'll watch the little motors down below... I never heard of this guy Crusoe, nor why he comes to mind when you see me. Croesus...? But I'll content you – being alone is good, until I'm hungry...'

*

'He won't have another revelation,' Julia says. 'They never do. It means the first one's just skin deep.'

'An accident,' Coralie agrees. 'No test, no metaphor. The charts, the winds – they send you to the rocks. Usually no one survives the storm – or there's illiteracy, no story, so we wouldn't know...'

'We've cast Pavel adrift,' says Julia. 'When the ship arrives – it isn't rescue: those guys will take him off to jail. But Coralie – my motive's scientific. How will he do, Pavel, use his peace, his poverty? Can you survive with nothing, then lose even that? So, Coralie – what's your motive? You're not vindictive, are you, dear?'

'If everyone deserts, if everybody draws their line...' Coralie starts...

'Oh dear,' says Julia. 'The sin of individualism? Not that again I hope, dear Coralie?'

'It's not to punish him, although he'll suffer – being on his own. I need a general principle...' says Coralie.

'Maybe there isn't one,' says Julia. 'It's like they say – we know more and more, until the knowledge that we started with is exhausted.'

'I don't see that, Julia,' says Coralie. 'We must go on with experiments, not flashes – surely, that is how you work? My plan is – reduce Pavel to nothing, a zero. Then see if there's a plus, a positive... A number, even: nationality ... a ninny-nanny...'

'Then we're agreed!' says Julia. 'You ask if Pavel will reach a goodness – I wonder what there is that isn't taught and beaten in...'

They drink to that. They run a tab ... and Pavel sneaks down to the street, and hops and cartwheels on his way...

★

'You must think of this as purgatory, Pavel,' Vito says. 'We're all guilty of something, and innocent of almost everything else. Waiting – that's the sentence. You are the prison of yourself. The law tells me nothing about you, Pavel, so there's no place for law in justice... Who knows, Pavel – you had it in for Cristiano, because he was making out with Lidia?'

'I wouldn't know,' says Pavel. 'It would be normal.'

'I'm dealing with real criminals,' says Vito. 'Not politicals, but guys who dedicate their lives to it.'

The table's covered in black plates and beakers. There's flags and posters – here laid out, there's a feast of mushrooms, stunted thick legs, caps cigar-brown – *funghi porcini*, shipped in from the Bosnian forest: not many celebrants sat in wait.

'There's some trick you do with milk and mushrooms – takes the venom out,' says Vito. 'I don't recall the detail. It's like snakes – you tempt them with a pomegranate, something like that, snatch it away, give them a branch to bite on. Out it comes, the malice...'

'It's cold here,' Pavel says. 'Am I staying with you, Vito?'

'Lidia was a golden girl, Pavel,' says Vito. 'You must have matched her colour with your own. She was solid, through and through – you were just painted on, Pavel.'

'She took me in,' says Pavel. 'She was a flame – could have burned the trees – but she went dumb, extinguished, back into the magic matchbox. Then we three went to rob the dead.'

'Yes, yes,' says Vito. 'I'd picked her out. Lidia was really mine.'

'I've nothing more to say,' says Pavel. 'You make it sound like Rashomon.'

'This place,' says Vito, 'we used to think it grew into America. Then there came the poverty – now, it's unrecognisable, not like itself and not like anywhere. Bits and pieces, nothing you would identify. It could be granny's shawl, buried in a wormy box, slipped into shreds...'

'Don't persecute me, Vito,' Pavel says. 'It isn't worth it. We're all frustrated for what we had and didn't have. I loved Cristiano, never harmed him...'

'Hmmmm,' says Vito. 'Your love ... it brings a desolation, Pavel. Everything about you. Blocks with no windows and the doors blown out – kids running to the camps pitched in the sand. That's you...'

'I'm free, Vito,' Pavel says. 'Almost. You use the law to get the guilty off, and common sense if you think they're innocent. It's a start – I've seen through the problematic stuff – the rights, the duties, the higher voice – all that. My problem is – the mind. It seems that if there is one, it depends on other things – outside or inside, who knows which. It seems to be original for every one, and so – you can't hazard general laws... Those two – Coralie and Julia – they wanted general principles, but then the drink took over... Each mind wandered its own way...'

'It's the peace,' says Vito. 'It makes you think of settling scores with those you hate, and running off. When there is war, it's hugger-mugger, murder's passed over, accounts suspended – philosophy transcended... Peace...'

'Oh,' Pavel says. 'That was just one guy, perched up on his horse.'

'Anyway,' says Vito, 'don't worry about your mind – you've a thalamus – it's never bothered you. It works, you don't need see where it is lodged – inside and outside, Pavel, it makes no sense.'

'Now there's peace,' says Pavel. 'You can't trust anyone. When there was a war, you could trust your side – but of course, I found I didn't have one. All the differences between people have gone – everyone's untrustworthy.'

'I have the answer,' Vito says. 'This area – I'm sure it had a Roman name. A republic? A free zone of some kind. This is an earthquake area...'

'It looks disturbed, like everywhere,' Pavel says. 'Dusty...'

'Oh, there hasn't been an earthquake yet,' says Vito. 'And I'm not yet a minister. That's a time, a probability, question. Like conflict and victory – at least, an armistice. Time's your measure in all that. You see, Pavel – I serve the law. That means I take cash from criminals to get them off – and – I show innocence for free. That is the best! I'm clean, and – I have the power.'

'This republic,' Pavel asks. 'How will you live?'

'Oh, we'll find a wonder underground, and dig it up, and charge a fee. Or else – we'll do what we used to do, we three, keep mum and sell the good stuff to our friends...'

'I see myself in that,' says Pavel. 'It's harmless fun...'

'Yes, Pavel,' Vito says. 'You won't be here. You homeless chancers – have no place in this. Better be chased off, than locked up. You'd maybe work for me, but that's not what you want...'

'There's two valid sorts of lives, Vito,' Pavel says. 'Each to be lived – by yourself alone, if you're versatile and hybrid, or most likely, by two people, two different sorts. The ancients – they were wrong. They wanted one theory of what we are, they thought there was a single "man", like – "Look! A lion! A horse!" Two types, Vito. First, there's what I am: the first man in the world, the universe. The last, too. Everything to me is new and irreproachable, with consequences unforeseeable ... extinction is the rule, survival is like musical chairs. All made for me, all mine, for my delight, my suffering – and my regret it can't go on... The walking up and down, the valleys, the trees... Then, there's the life you're living now – in the pot, the plot, trying everything that's been tried, the dull, the scuffed, reading the law reports, scheming, seceding, irrigating sick guys, shooting the escapees ... writing, lecturing, promulgating. Inventing pastimes. Tiny tunnels. Blancoing your anklets.

That's a valid life too, Vito, just like mine. You don't need lots of science to see that; the philosophy is simple too...'

'If there's two ways valid, why not an infinity?' asks Vito.

'I put it in terms that you can understand,' Pavel says.

'There's another difference,' Vito says. 'I live on, in the collective body. You, Pavel, disappear. Your remains are dumped, dump in the dump. The Etruscans – they only seem to disappear because they went into the history. The mystery. Or maybe they were stolen, got resurrected. They're here, in all of us. They are my type, Pavel. They had a context, gods, ambitions, wives and kids.'

'Oh,' says Pavel, 'that's vainglory, Vito. You'll linger on, perhaps, shut in a scroll. I'll be a spirit, misty, gas... I'll go in the air, for sure. You'd breathe me in, like pollen, bug eggs, viruses – or night stocks. You'll never know: I'm perfume, Vito.'

'That comes from your past, Pavel,' Vito says, with some disdain. 'A fiction, snide, irreverent. Leskov, I bet. The twisted Russian soul that scurries like a hank of dust around your foot – then bites your ankle, cocks its snook...'

'That isn't me at all,' says Pavel. 'The Russians – when you need them most they come ... at other times ... you hope they won't...'

'I need,' says Vito. 'To find some thing enormous. A necropolis. Sweep all these huts away...' and he waves towards the stone houses on the slope, some with violet stucco painted on. 'No one will live here now. I need a show. And guards. Protecting, armed. Marauding too, if there's some trade that doesn't suit...'

'You'd need some frescoes,' Pavel says. 'Just holes – they don't attract.'

'Oh, we can deal with that,' says Vito. 'There's guys who're trained to spruce things up.'

'You know,' Pavel says. 'There's something brings us two together – when we were here, the three of us. Cristiano's death – absurd, it seems to me, sinister it seems to you. Remember the cat, the guy who loved it so much he couldn't bear to think it died... Somewhere it still purrs...'

'Schroder?' asks Vito. 'It's false. Not so. The cat is dead.'

'Suppose there were some cops – proper ones, not like here: space cops,' says Pavel. 'Maybe with informers all through the universe – who could be with Cristiano in the instant before his death – identifying who did it... Perched on a rock somewhere, spying into everybody's time. That would satisfy you, Vito,' Pavel says.

'If that were so,' says Vito, 'they'd need be there, those super sleuths, all dead and all alive, on rocks, in clouds of gas, all over everywhere, before the fact, and during it. They could have intervened. Warned, stopped the violence. Parleyed. No one was there, Pavel, except who did it, no one else saw.'

'OK, Vito,' Pavel says. 'Now you know. You should be satisfied. That's peace, Vito.'

'No, Pavel,' says Vito. 'That's paranoia. No cops. Some things happen no one sees.'

'Don't laugh, Vito,' Pavel says. 'Remember – "The Trojan war will not take place" – and then it does. That's Russian for you...'

'Except it's not,' says Vito, irritated. 'It happened. We weren't there. We can't stop the Trojan war, Pavel, goddam it!'

'There's surveillance, Vito,' Pavel says. 'You know that. Armed and everywhere.'

'Trojans,' says Vito. 'Now you're talking! If one found them, the whole cast, all dressed up...'

*

'There's danger they can twist discovery into dystopias, Pavel,' says Vito. 'We must be careful ... museums, stuffed kittens, roundabouts...'

'You wouldn't dig up your relatives,' says Pavel. 'Round here – they're all your relatives.'

'Oh, I don't know so much, Pavel,' says Vito. 'They're quite reduced, the lot of them. What's special about the road you trudge along, Pavel, that gives you insight into everything?'

'It always changes,' Pavel says. 'No insight. It's all fresh, hard, and resistant. Some guys live from poems and the tales we travellers hear each day... Not worth a cent! It takes them sitting in their sweat in offices to print out what we hum all day...'

'You leech, Pavel,' says Vito. 'Your feet will rot off.'

'There's Lidia. Coralie – they had some fun,' says Pavel. 'Even at my expense. When I deserted, that wasn't how I'd intended it. But you can hoe all day, and weevils get the lot.'

'But still you eat, Pavel,' Vito says.

'How angry are you, Vito?' Pavel asks.

'Oh, not with you especially – it's just your sort,' Vito says. 'You're sludge. You think that after an epiphany you can be holy monks, and sell revelations as a horror movie script. It will not work, Pavel. You are banal, a passenger. You say what everybody knows. You hate the cops – but they are there because of you...'

'And do we cause the wars as well?' asks Pavel.

'You're in the crowd – you cheer, you love to loot, you fight like clowns, then when you lose – there's protests,' Vito says. 'There is no revelation. Everything is ending somewhere every day, and soon – into the darkness we go down... our flaking desiccated lips won't ever use those beakers, scoff olives from black platters in our tombs ...'

'Well,' Pavel says, 'we can agree on that.'

'So...' says Vito.

'So, my sort caused the death of Cristiano,' Pavel says.

'At last!' says Vito. 'We've arrived! You called him, up the perilous track. But he deserved the beating. He was greedy and imprudent. You're not forgiven, Pavel. But it doesn't matter. He didn't have a clue. He was a dullard, and later the epiphany was yours. A flash in your skull pan. Enjoy it.'

'You need a realm, Vito,' Pavel says. 'On your own – it doesn't count.'

'I'll make me one,' says Vito. 'That way we'll face the moral question – violence, all that ... it doesn't seem to trouble you, Pavel...'

'It wasn't present,' Pavel says. 'Perhaps somewhere much higher up, they settled it.'

'Here,' says Vito. 'I'm higher up. They'll come for me with laws. That's embarrassing. Then – with arms – that's the conundrum.'

★

'If you make a Konya,' Pavel says. 'The perfect place, I'll be with you. I – anyone – could be happy there.'

'You're a dualist, Pavel,' Vito says. 'There's a here and there, before and after, for you. It's all one thing then another, your head, your groin – a fumbling two step. Maybe even right and wrong – that was your epiphany, after all. You just can't make anything of it. Your twins unholy – fall about, they're shackled, even Siamese ... There's the something that you roam in, and the nothing that awaits. You yesterday, another you tomorrow. Interpretation: love, sentiments, the songs – all opalescent, a shimmer on the wings. I'm different. I want it all at once. If I must compromise and chivvy – it's still mine, a unity. I'm a visionary, it's still mine to construct. I'm not a visionary, Pavel, but I have a vision. It all fits, it's a machine, producing nothing, being everything. You're not a priority of mine, my friend, but chatting with you changes my position, makes it coherent, more unyielding...'

'The tombs, Vito... And the friendship,' Pavel says.

'All one, Pavel. The landscape, the continent – they will split again, but earth, the ball, the hot patty sailing round – that's one, and all the beasts that danced and roared – all into loam, all mulch with ornaments... And friends – they think they're counsellors – but they just help me to define my path. The guys that killed Cristiano – who connived – maybe we'll punish them... So what? A friend has gone – the murderers, they're not new friends. Cool eyes, Pavel – it's not an ad, it's what you need... One day I'll maybe have to ride the horse, and do my rounds...'

'You're puffed up, Vito,' Pavel says. 'You're just a piece of grit in someone's shoe...'

'It's maybe so,' says Vito. 'That is why I need to start from small. Compact.'

*

'What are we sitting on, Pavel?' Vito asks.

'Earth, Vito,' says Pavel. 'Like what all the past is buried in, the bone and ash, male and female, beast and fish, worm and snake... All silted down, and all enclosed. Above, the blue, the fug, the mist... We have no choice,' says Pavel. 'We sit upon the earth. Like we do now.'

'Yes, Pavel,' Vito says. 'And what do people like?'

'Visits from guys who do not stay. A game of cards, a dance with someone else's girl, a punchup and a feast,' says Pavel, feeling pushed along... 'The food, so good the first time, everything loved and longed for so far back, first times of everything – the kiss, the roast, the dawn...'

'This earth,' Vito goes on. 'Does it seem to you an animal? Or something else?'

'A mother, or an elephant? No,' says Pavel, humouring Vito. 'It's too big, inert – life comes from it, but it isn't life.'

'Oh come on, Pavel!' Vito shouts. 'This takes a year! It's a machine, you fool. A machine like they have all over, that dispenses stuff – the coca and the contraceptive, air for your tires, ticket to ride, your cash... It's a machine, you cretin, that pours out minerals you never heard of, jewels you stick on your ears and nose, gas for your motors...'

'It's evident,' says Pavel. 'In a way. On it goes. Keeping people out, punishing the thieves, eating the nursery food ... copulation, rites, then down you go ... into the machine. Until it runs out, of course. But even then, it still spins on, maybe who's left, right till the end, still has epiphanies; the horsemen are the only ones who're left, but they ride on...'

'Yes, yes,' says Vito. 'Forget them – you won't know. Think amusement, Pavel, replication, miniatures. Some guys set up what they call Russian mountains: *montagne russe*. Those rides that tear your belly out and show you how your plane will crash. Some guys are still on Mickey Mouse. Others are fixed on Noah's Ark, or parks for animals. What is the best though, dear Pavel, – is an earth. A home. Where they can eat the food they love, the pasta and the artichokes: play *tresette,* hear the melodrama... All over, done with; it's been tried. All that's on offer, as a permanent alternative is what you cling to: your Homeland. Nothing extraneous, just familiar things, and fuck the rest. Indigenes all, who know the tunes, the rules... Respect, all that.'

'Your plan? You're going to make a little earth for people here?' asks Pavel, amazed. 'An earth that's made of earth? And spins? You sit on it, round it goes, there's room to fornicate and die and harvest plums ... with crows and seagulls...'

'Right!' says Vito. 'All exactly so – except no seagulls, and no sea. What a waste! A lake, perhaps. A tank of fish. But cover all that ground with salty spew – crazy stuff, Pavel!'

'Forgive me, Vito,' Pavel says. 'I understand the guys and what they crave – "Beer and Love", "America Bar": it has its resonance. Just – it seems quite fuddy-duddy.'

'If you don't suit,' says Vito. 'Like you, Pavel, you don't: – or if you're young, a loner – you can get off.'

'... And it's made of...?' Pavel asks.

'Earth, what else. Earth made of earth – stones and all,' says Vito. 'No satellite, no colonies, no extra planets. It'll be just like all those other countries, looking for their rationale, their uniqueness, their compactness... You have them everywhere, on every continent. My earth secedes – but it's tiny, homely. Doesn't threaten. Law-abides.'

'What's in it for you, Vito?' Pavel asks.

'It's my creation,' Vito says. 'Better than a flat country with a fence. My little earth will spin, on the same principles the big one does. In a way, I'll be the boss. But it won't be tough, like countries when there's promiscuity... There, you check, you balance, there is hate and endless fiddling with the ins and outs... My earth, which we can add to – another load of topsoil does the trick – is what you'd call a paradise...'

'It's your epiphany,' says Pavel. 'A big idea. Lidia would fit in well... Not Cristiano, though.'

'No,' says Vito. 'Lidia's a natural – Cristiano was a sloth – not when it came to cash... He'd tramp the big world for a job...'

Pavel's excited – by the new world he's already been deported from...

'La belle époque,' says Vito. 'You start to cry, even at the sound. And then, you know – it all falls down... The actresses, the tarts, the painters – my God! – time's on the stairs, he brings them rancid glands, their metabolism's up the spout ... the coughs, the bleeds, brown spots...'

'I know all that,' says Pavel. 'Explain your earth. The suspension, the spin... How do you manage that?'

'Of course,' says Vito, 'you don't know the internet. You need to worm your way, then when you find the sign, you stake your pot. Of course, it must be customised... Cash terms. There's always been a trade in earths. In the past, it was just metaphor... second suns, "you are my sunshine..." remember that? The moons – you'll have read it somewhere, at the start in China there were seven of them. The East, Pavel! The stars, the sun, the moon – they weren't alien, stuff in the sky through glass, they were more intimate, they doubled up, they multiplied ... that star, if you recall, your woman, who's presentable – "when only one is shining in the sky" – is that how it goes? One star! – never in science, of course, but in poetry, on silk in the bazar – as many as you like, as few ... a hunter's moon, that big red face: a blue cheese moon, grinning like a Cheshire cat – gorgonzola, that's for sure... Oh yes – spin, it will. The difference is – the horizon. It will be so close – no longer will it be – "somewhere over the rainbow" – you'll see where rainbows end, where the gold, the pyrites or whatever, where it is. You just need dig. Maybe you'll find ... who knows.'

'Those songs,' says Pavel. 'I could do without.'

'You must enter in,' says Vito. 'It's the spirit you must offer up. You'd be the guy who doesn't want to go to heaven because the company's dull.'

'It may be so,' says Pavel. 'Everybody'd know everything. Nothing to talk about.'

'That's right, Pavel,' Vito says. 'It's not your thing. You could leave now. You're a savage once again.'

'I've not learned much from you, Vito,' Pavel says. 'You're like my epiphany – just a flash. You can desert without one...'

'My new world,' says Vito. 'Has a purpose and beginning. Something's gone wrong round here, these countries, that is clear, and everybody knows. We'll start again – not from right back – just a step away. You'll see – we'll be happy, living in the right way, according to the law.'

'You're right,' Pavel says. 'It's not for me. You're thirsty for marauding, Vito: once you're established, safe ... you'll see. They'll punish you.'

'The seeing will be mine,' says Vito. 'More than you can say of it, Pavel: you don't decide a thing – it just streams past. And – I don't maraud: I trade, and I negotiate and bargain. I'm a homebody, my friend – keep off!'

As Pavel leaves, someone's coming in. 'Good luck, Lidia,' Pavel doesn't say.

*

'This is France,' says Gaston. 'They watch you more carefully here than where you came from.'

'Everywhere I go,' says Pavel. 'I feel more free. The horsemen are fewer – riding's just for fun or show.'

There's a friendly fire to sit around, a shadowy room, bottles and pricelists...

'Should I know about this guy Vito?' Gaston asks. 'His world?'

'Earth,' says Pavel. 'Not world. He doesn't study, doesn't read: it's interesting only if it falls apart. Mud to mud...'

'That's a safe bet,' Gaston says. They rest their feet.

'If those are *crabes au gratin*, Gaston,' says Pavel, as the other starts to eat. 'I'm hungry; I'm sorry for the animals, of course...'

'You say that about everyone,' says Gaston, cleaning shells out with a stick. 'Now – being a deserter, Pavel – that's not so original. Being a sculptor, as you say ... a minor art. Nature's not been beaten by your hammering ... Now it isn't only fame and innocence you want – it's food!'

'No contest, with my carving!' Pavel says. 'Nature sculpts much bigger blocks. A joust with nature was never quite my thing.'

'I could share my crabs, Pavel,' says Gaston. 'If you've brought along a woman I could share with you.'

'No,' says Pavel. 'Women are well, and well without me. This plastic laundry bag is all I own.'

'It could be more than just a bag – it looks heavy, full of cash,' says Gaston. 'Anything smallish? Worth a million? Or loaded and well-oiled?'

'I'm still hungry,' Pavel says.

'You're a prisoner,' says Gaston. 'Guys like you. The sacred canopy, all is one, pre-ordained, everyone the same except for their gender, their obedience – it's a cupola. What you do, should do, other people too – laws and destinies, ghosts and foetuses: here it comes, the order, clangour of the word! Mouthed by dinosaurs.'

'Oh no,' says Pavel, 'I don't believe in dinosaurs.'

'Well, that's something, that's a start,' says Gaston, handing Pavel slices of smoked goose. 'No one goes along with that, the unity, wherever they are from. It's broken, there's just the daily orders.'

'You live well here,' says Pavel. 'I thought I was the transgressive one. Not voting, not laying up a treasure... There must be some angle, some low trade, to run a place like this. And you're a laugh, Gaston, a star. You've some vocabulary too!'

'Don't wear out your cells in cogitating,' says Gaston. 'Be reassured: some wars are real, not play. And – some horsemen are to be believed. Don't puzzle any more – the violence is over. Now, if you feel like it – sex can begin. That war? Yours, you call it – it's finished, Pavel. Nothing lasts for ever, there has to be a deal, the victims counted, a trial. It's over, we can have our feast. You've done well, Pavel, by yourself – no killing, no terrorism, not even looting. It's amazing how you've passed your time while others suffered, said they were bringing suffering to its end – with you, hardly suffering at all. Your feet did, possibly...'

'No one would have benefited if I had suffered terribly,' Pavel says.

'Most people are hypocrites, Pavel, and disagree with that – but I am sure you're right,' Gaston says. 'Anyway, your road – Damascus, epiphany... You'll know how many other roads there are to walk on, so many capitals, epiphanies for each. Revelations, possibly. I'll show you round, now you've done this stretch – the mule track that you took... Try to take the views in silently, not dwelling on what everybody knows, pointing at the monuments in awe.'

'We need some beer to wash this down,' says Pavel, finishing off the goose. 'So, it's peace – just like the horseman said. I don't believe it, not a word, but still, it's possible you don't believe a word I say, and that's the basis of the deal we'd make. My fortune – could grow here with you...'

'It's dark now, Pavel,' says Gaston. 'I can't show you what lies beneath, what drives the landscape – the meaning of the signs and images imprinted on the scene – those turrets on the mansion over there, their tiles like scales on pangolins – an upscale club, a hydro, where we could eat some more, had you the cash. Then, there's the olive groves, afar, a hoary chestnut, one cicada calling, and the sea – right now it's black of course, or maybe just invisible ... but full of life you wouldn't want to meet when it's alive...'

'That poor goose ... but, it was good,' says Pavel.

'Well,' says Gaston. 'Let the good goose repose. You don't see bad people here, do you?'

'I don't see anyone,' Pavel says.

'With the sun, comes the detail,' says Gaston. 'But with peace – there's fewer poor guys on the move – I told you, it's like musical chairs...'

'I heard that,' Pavel says. 'But not from you.'

'There's a band round here,' Gaston presses on. 'Though we don't do the music. Maybe,' and he laughs. 'We stack the chairs. Among the things we do is thieve. Forget the good and bad, think context. Judge by what you see, the peace here, the striving, the companionship. You're from the East. Coming here – it must have toughened you. A sturdy type, and fancy free. Free to fly, and hover like a bee. You'd fit right in – it's expected of you. This landscape – it's full of fancy too. There for the taking, when the detail and the daylight come, and you can see good people with their goods...'

'I've never robbed the living,' Pavel says. 'We used to rob the dead, but that was a philosophy. We were against the fetishism of the past, and sought to make a buck from our dissent...'

'It sounds perverse to me,' says Gaston. 'You're free not to come along with us, of course. But then your suffering would start again... On principle, you're against the hurt. I'd sympathise, but hurt is part of everything. We're all grown rich from past endeavours, copying, stealing the first thoughts – some of our creations are artistic, even if it's only moving things about on stage. I cite your chiselling, Pavel... Your challenge to the past! What we do, I shouldn't call it anarchy: we're organised and reasonable: after all, if you want smoked goose, you don't attack the chef... We don't impose ideas on anyone, no territorial plans, no appeal to history, nor a book – quite the contrary. We don't want people thinking our thoughts, no building watchtowers, writing about us... I see myself as oakum, the stuff the prisoners picked to plug the planks and keep the boat afloat... Modest and unassertive.'

'Sailing on clichés,' Pavel says. 'That boat.'

'You Easterners,' laughs Gaston. 'Your languages are hard to read and write. With some purpose, I suppose. Hiding, dissembling, is your speciality. We too aren't passionate about the modern, its transparent brevity. Like my grannie – she stood up to pray and knelt to sing! Those alphabets! Writing with the left! The uncertainties of tense! Well, you can forget all that. Not needed. Not if you come in with us.'

'That's not me...' Pavel starts. 'I can write the Roman way.'

'Maybe you think ours is just the wrong side,' Gaston says. 'You're lucky – most people don't know they're on it, the bad side. Most sides, good ones too, they have bad people. Or no one knows: those Asian wars... India... China... You've seen it all from the inside, Pavel. Where did it all lead to? What did it give you? Lidia? Sponging off those women, drinking to excess ... conniving at illegality? Was that the good? Did you find love? Vito...? His dusty rustic ball? Now, you're at the end. You can't cover your experiences by saying you want a new state, more laws, more rigor, even less. More land?... Now, you could be the good person, fighting on the wrong side... Maybe after all, you can reason it all out – good or bad, that's not a side...

Leave aside the awkward bits. When you went to rob the dead, it wasn't a campaign ... just, kind of fun...?'

'Is this the moment when we see what epiphany was for...?' asks Pavel.

'"Not for anything", was what you said,' says Gaston.

'All right,' says Pavel, 'we've established – you're robbing people. Do you call it politics? Justice? You're not Nazis, it's just another Trojan war, not really necessary, but grey and big, something you'd not do without, when it's gone by. A war you sing along with. Social banditry: that is your thing, your logic ... you needn't do it, but for you, Gastard, it's your amber room, your golden temple ... after the big battle, you've laid down an epic.'

'No battle,' Gaston says. 'This here's a *guinguette* – a disco before discos. We dance, we drink.'

'A thieves' kitchen?' Pavel asks.

'No kitchen,' Gaston says. 'Booze and dance, "Beer and love", you might say. And, Pavel – this could be your spot. And me – I could be, well, anything you like. I saw you struggling up the track, I thought, "here's someone, could be anyone"...'

'I'm here or anywhere – to seek my fortune,' Pavel says. 'Not company... Keep your distance, Gaston: I didn't do well with women – I don't feel like trying it with men...'

*

It looks like dawn is here. There's groups of people sitting round – they must be residents: – women giving him the eye, and men the scowl. It's all as things were, like when Pavel started out...

'I've been through all of this,' he says.

'No!' says Gaston. 'It's true, you look like the eternal on its circuit – you're like a beast who's burrowed out from its archaic tomb... Things have changed now, Pavel. Good and bad – they change their place, their face. Big crime is art. Bosses have class. That must be what I – we – want. Who dreams of ending small?'

'If yours isn't crime then,' Pavel says. 'Why give it that unlovely name?'

'You're right, Pavel,' says Gaston. 'It's ordinary, banal. It's everyday. Just spectacle. Look into my eyes, Pavel...'

'There's two coiled things, like salamanders, Gaston,' Pavel says.

'One thing used to lead to another,' says Gaston, pressing on. 'Now, it's just photos – I don't allow them here. A frozen snap! We're all waiting for our fortunes to arrive. So, there must be a chain, events, Pavel: leading to more events.'

The band of robbers sings softly, there's an accordion – 'Misty'.

'Those salamanders,' Gaston says, holding tight on Pavel's arm, to twist him round towards the view. 'Do you see me as a Valois? That was the sort of king you'd want to be – his badge, like mine, the salamander. I live in the fire, Pavel. Those old types – ordinary people, living lives quite different from ours. They knew how to cover up ... campaigns, deaths, massacres. Their scenery – the chase, the bible, in gold thread hanging on the wall. Remember the poet – "the flame, a bridge of fire between the real and the unreal, coexistence of being and non-being". Dreams – I've learnt to live with them, ignoring them. And for you, Pavel – those presidents, the tsars and sultans, the imams and the kings – what was their scenery? You saw it all – torn and broken, those scumbled flats, the glassless windows, doorless doors: cement wafted into dust. What a mess, what dirty settings! I don't want immortal life, Pavel – I'm not at all religious. But I want a life that's long enough ... that I can say "enough". "I made it!" Or – "I made some of it, or none..." That's all a salamander expects. So, are you one of us? Fireproof? Doing what I say? You surely don't want someone precious, whimsical?' he asks, squeezing Pavel's upper arm.

'I don't want anyone at all,' Pavel says. 'Roaming is my trade, profession. You can't pick up just anyone along the way...'

'That's important,' Gaston says, holding him at arm's length, scrutinising, blowing breath into his face. 'What you just said. Jollity and danger – you don't feel at home, although that's what you've had and what you want... Good! You're right. Forget the photos and the spectacles, forget me, and all the rest you've seen and – run!'

'You and me?' says Pavel, fearfully. 'Together?'

'No, Pavel,' says Gaston, waving an iron-shod stave at him. 'I misjudged you, and myself. Just run! Begone. Practise your trade, and roam!'

★

Gaston pushes him down the hill – the prickly bushes, spiders in the dewy dawn, claggy outcroppings of clay, some asters, thistles, aloes.

'For certain, it's my vision,' Pavel thinks. 'Lets me down. I could have prospered even here. People, love, and innovation – they slip away, and I am glad. That epiphany – what a curse, it sets me out there in the wild, beyond the palisade. A seer who doesn't see. Suppose – nothing was revealed. Mere firing in the brain – an episode, a flash ... a fire, a presage of consuming flame, the whole grey sog inflammable, then becoming ash and cinder, leaving a blackened nut inside the skull...'

*

Down on the plain, there's cowboys – guys on horses, waving long wood spears. They shouldn't be here in this spot, 'holà'-ing, but there they are – quite characteristic, galloping around.

'One of those horsemen,' Pavel thinks. 'Could be the one, the one that's special, different, that we're waiting for.'

3

INTERLUDE

I N THEIR MIDDLE AGES, two men, their minds rich, their flipflops poor – on their perches, dust, or even sand, around...

'...something like a switch, in part of the brain we usually don't enter; if you turn it, it's immortality! No ageing!' Musa says.

'But still death, if you don't watch out?' Choban asks.

'Decapitation? – yes, I dare say.'

'Stasis, though,' says Choban. 'Innovation has no in or out. Unchanging youthfulness – but round about, how would everything change, always? Is death the great creator?'

'There's the children you don't want to have. That's mortality, the proof, the end,' says Musa.

'...Not eating with me, an offence, a blessing,' says Choban. 'Getting high by themselves.'

'Anyway, let's talk of people we know who deserve a death,' says Musa. 'Not doing it, bringing it on, would be grave, an omission. The means are chancy. To every prey, its margin of escape. There's always tenderness – crows rolling in the snow. The net is fine – you catch the little fish. The big ones make a hole and bolt.'

'Will you do those operations?' Choban asks. 'And will our countries take us?'

'I'm not licensed. I got the gold medal, but as I took it, on the stage, my hand was shaking,' says Musa. 'So – I'm not a doctor now.'

'I don't want a country, I want a place – a line of black hills, flame rising, hares in a field of flowers,' Choban says.

'Yes – red, white and blue flowers – could be France, Holland, Russia or the States. I've been waiting ten years... you?'

'Oh, I'm not a refugee, or displaced,' says Choban. 'I'm just looking. My war is over – I can't return, no one loves me there.'

'It's fancy, comes from sitting here – that one day someone comes and lifts you somewhere else, gives you a room, and off you start again,' says Musa. 'No one's resentful, or afraid – you do exactly what you want, fulfil your plan...'

'It's not exaggerated,' Choban says. 'Unlikely: but the world is full of holes, a net that lets some through – the modest and the angry – even me.'

'Why not?' says Musa. 'Chance visits here. There's plans and errors – you must wait, in go the numbers – the safe door opens...' and he makes the sign of someone taking cash unlimited...

'When they ask you here – they don't care about your politics, still less philosophy. If you don't want to bomb them, they give a passing grade,' he says.

'Some of us got bombed,' says Choban. 'They did it, those people doing interviews. I wasn't there. They showed it on TV – cadavers. I can't claim persecution, or anything at all.'

★

The officer stops running. It's his time to interrogate. Now, the turn of one of the mature men, sitting on their spot. This one – not so old and mature after all ... could even be aggressive, or sneaky. That's what the inquisitor must reveal.

'Listen,' says the officer, sweaty in his cotton top – his badge says 'Vito': 'Choban. You can choose a genre. Horror, snuff, magic, or sci-fi... Even sentimental schluck. That's the norm. Spin your tale, tale your spin! But what I need, what will assist you – isn't genre. It's coming out to me as someone with feelings just like mine, a destiny involving me, a fate that sucks me in. Something authentic, that lasts, with memorable scenes... In this journey, you must earn the next step. Now, you're a pawn – you could be crowned. Convince me – and I'll put you on the bus.'

'That's genre too,' says Choban. 'It's the bang of the bourgeois, their cannon, the harpoon to the whale. Greatworks. I can't do it. It ends good, it ends bad ... if it makes you cry, it's a success. I don't know how I end, and if you cry – too bad for you. Except – you enjoy feeling the feel, you need it, like wanting ice-cream in the sun. Emotion, for people far away, on the page or on the screen.'

He thinks how he could take the officer's place: even his shoes would fit. The jogging's out, but – remember – take the badge, you're Vito. One more murder, fold the body into two... Dumped behind the cabinet...

'You're lucky,' says the officer. 'You get an interview, to see if someone wants you: some country, nothing personal. You have to bring out something good, that somebody might want. If I say you don't leave, then here in the zombieland you stay. It could be even longer, before you're asked again. This is not a camp, you're not confined – it's living scrabbling poor for ever. Being poor means you're settled in your destiny. Destitute – means you might be on the move.'

'So, it could be ten more years before I'm seen again?' Choban asks.

'If you're lucky,' says the officer. 'It sounds like something from long long past, those Thirties plays, of people waiting – frontiers, consuls, "play it again", last boats – all that. But as they say, "bad things only change to better things". This time around – you're not in danger. Quite the reverse. If you're on the move – that's different. Risk cuts in again. That must be what you want. Something to happen, something you think is in my gift.'

'There's my surgeon friend,' says Choban: 'Musa. Make him tranquil, he'll perform. Take him instead...'

'That would be disaster,' Vito says. 'Living for ever, if you're careful. Don't you see the tent-pole? – it's dying: everything is, quite quick. It always does. We don't want more people, older ones, who think they're wise – everything is known. What you can't do – it's immaterial: it's still known. What's to come that we don't already have? You're a harmless type, Choban, stale cake. Go! Be grateful, don't complain, don't organise. No underground, no equality, no saying no. People move, or they are pushed. Why not you, a wonderful country waiting like a glove to hold your life... There's the bus outside. Don't thank me – run!'

★

Last on the bus, the last seat, can't see outside...

'It's a strange life,' says Choban to the guy beside. 'Ours. But ordinary, normal. No one has lived up to what they should, their destiny. The leaders – incompetent and superficial: and where have all the workers gone? Missed their big scene ... drinking out the back. Surprised they were let down...? Now you've the choice: priests and imams, who say the final judgment's imminent, and all the rest who say that everything is imminent, but there's no judgment to await.'

The guy beside him makes out he's asleep.

One of the nights they've travelled, the guy must have got off. Good: he's disappeared, there's room.

Here's the place. A town? A country?

★

'Choban?' asks another officer: 'Romanian? Chechen? Don't you have another name?'

'Bruce would do,' says Choban. 'Scottish.' You think quick, when you're interrogated, then you do it all again, and better, when it's done.

The chief is the chief. No one recognises him, he has another name. Not Choban now – Bruce, Robert. And smelly clothes. The ragged soldier on the desk, his loyal foot-soldier – serves him – and out of some sense of raggedness ... perceives the lustre, the epic person, not the travesty. The chief – has to be hidden, can't live in the fortress... You don't need servants, there is just the single room. You don't need take the crap job. You're the chief. It happens to each one, Choban thinks, it's the commonplace of chiefs. Though – you and the ragged squaddy, are both nonenties, but that is history too...

'It's not much,' says the ragged soldier. 'Best you live hidden. If you feel grateful, you needn't say so.'

'I might,' says Choban. 'Stay concealed. Be grateful. But that is not my part. No, not at all.'

*

There's working through all this, the detail: the scene will change, another act...

'You've been reluctant to let me in here,' says Choban. 'It must mean here's a tough place to live. Where I came from, they fitted you in, the extra ones, a crack in their wall, like a gecko or a snake. It was normal, expected of them: not a delight, of course. A blessing, they used to say. Heavy, those are heavy, blessings...'

This officer's a mother type – chubby, proud and ignorant, you'd want her in your family.

'The Colosseum – and those animals!' she says. 'None were killed there – think of the expense! It was all guys dressed in suits. A real fierce beast would not put on a show – the humans had to. As for your war – it was a little one, hardly a dustcloud in our retromirror. If it's not worldwide, just a rehearsal – all there's to do is sort the shards – like you, Choban. We might glue you, make a crooked pot...'

'I'm not that,' Choban says. 'Not a beaten soldier. I don't want to be senator, or emperor. I don't want what I can't be. But you can't put me with the animals, a dressing-up of tails and horns, led out to someone's sword. I can be anything that pays.'

'You're a dodger,' says the officer – maybe she's not the second mother – maybe she's the cook who makes a human stew. 'Dodgers don't get paid – they pay. You dodged your war – others will come. They're playing winner takes all – no one is smart enough to win the pot and take it home, and brick it up... You have to spend what you have won, the cash goes round so fast it heats ... and there you are again! Some plotters in a room will bring the cavalry, and in the pit the people go, hundreds and thousands. That's where peace flowers, Choban ... on the charnel pits... "a strong white flower".'

'You're there to stop that, officer,' says Choban, 'killing.'

'I'm not a cop,' says the second mother. 'I'm a humanitarian. I don't care if you're a communist. Or if there's religion, even some French philosophy. It doesn't count – besides, you have your plan.'

'That's what Musa said,' says Choban. 'He was my friend.'

The lady – or maybe it's her office – has a scent: there's a smell of sawdust, fresh-cut two-by-twos – a butcher's shop from long ago ... soaking up the blood of hares, dripping off their noses, snagged on the rack, shot and split, still leaping and screaming in the wild fields, one of the animals that cry, you don't know which. They cry for what we cry for but other things beside, things you don't understand, so you don't identify the species, nor cry with them...

'You mustn't hurt anybody, that is all,' the mother says. 'Whatever's been done to you, or you have done. You're born anew, remember.'

'Honest because I'm poor,' says Choban. 'You can be rich and honest – generous, at least, back where I was. Poverty's the price of honesty; I'm free and no one hears my voice – I feel I've made a great mistake...'

At her door, she shouts, 'Listen – you don't need be honest, just because you're poor.'

*

'Have some cider,' says the lady on the bench.

'Why not?' says Choban.

'That's a paradox,' the lady says. 'I tell you to do something, and you see it as a choice. Drink! It's not an argument. It's like: I don't believe in God – so what I don't believe in: is God. This cider – it's natural, but isn't made of apples. It's wine and vodka, and some codeine too. Drink up what's left, then go and buy the makings of some more. Use your imagination – it doesn't need always to be made the same.'

'That's your freedom thrown away,' says Choban. 'Passed on to me as my choice. and that's another paradox

– you get your freedom, and then you're responsible for it, the consequences... It's not freedom if you have to guess at unintended consequences, or the ones you hope ... or fear...'

'And not just that,' the lady says. 'It's better not go down that path. People get burnt for paradoxes – best stick to one set of rules, and so you're free.'

'That's what Musa said,' says Choban. 'We used to sit like this – upon a bench, the view is limitless.'

'You came out from talking to those cops,' the lady says. 'Born again? Means you'll have two deaths, at least.'

'No,' Choban says. 'That's casuistry.'

'You're starting bad,' the lady says. 'Drinking with me. I am the best, but I'm no use to you.'

'This codeine,' Choban says. 'Peace. Away with fear...'

'You need no faith,' the lady says, agreeing. 'A cup, perhaps, will help. Sharing a bottle, drinking from the neck with a stranger – that's a tabu.'

'You're not a stranger now,' says Choban. 'Though I don't know what you have become...'

'Questions,' says the lady. 'We've got down to those, like explorers, scientists – they look up at the stars, like me. Are there inhabitable rocks up there? I don't care! But. "Yes," they say, or maybe "no". Depends what living is. They'll never trek there, but they can have conversations with the stars, like the one we're having now... And here's a question for you: I need to doss down in the room you've been allotted. Does that seem good to you?'

'You're good with questions,' Choban says, swigging away.

The codeine ... no, he thinks. This is not the way to start.

'Of course,' he says. 'Peace! Just for a night...'

'The definition, here on earth,' the lady says. 'Of life – is what can die. So if we find a world that's dead – we've found life, our fault is – we arrived too late.'

'For sure it is our fault,' says Choban. 'Maybe we already bombed or poisoned it...'

'Quite so,' the lady says, taking off some socks. They cuddle down and sleep.

It's quite the wrong way to make a start, Choban thinks. Madeleine!

Dawn – not quite. She wakes. The lady's young and beautiful – quite naturally: no obsession here with appearances or gender stereotypes...

'You need to find a job,' says Madeleine. 'Why did they bring you here?'

'I was in need,' says Choban.

'It doesn't work like that,' says Madeleine. 'You look harmless. They have to let a number in. Me – I'm not dependable – but I might metamorph. Remember, Choban, I can tell you all you need to know. If you need more – ask someone with a telephone.'

There isn't much to eat.

'You're so lucky, Choban,' says Madeleine. 'In your eyes, there is the steppe, there's buildings always open, with truths written on the walls, the market – full of red silk and gold, ospreys and mynahs, semurghs as well, I bet... All solid, stable. What richness, Choban.'

'They don't like it if you're not there to buy, or follow an example, pray,' Choban says. 'Don't think to leech on me.

Here's our odd case: two's more defenceless than each one alone.'

'I know your sort,' says Madeleine. 'The more you know, the more it all must make a sense, a world of senses – and you, Choban, all the same, will think it makes no sense at all. We need some cash. The market here, you see it in the street – is not the real market. The real market's one you won't get in. You need a suit, avidity. You need the faith – observe the force, the earth moves... Market – it's an earthquake never still. But down there in the street, they sell stuff, red and green, and you can be a porter. Take some codeine: they're hiring guys, it's not yet dawn. Quick – the light drives all hope away... I'll wait...'

He doesn't see her for some days: 'I wouldn't leech on you,' she says. 'But, Choban, you're quite hopeless. Don't tell me how they took the room away because they saw me there – it isn't worthy of you. You're gold, Choban. An eviction – that's merely tailings, dross. You attract the persecution. It shows you're holy. We should make some interesting friends who'll help you go where you ought to be. Another room...'

Choban hefts the crates of rutabagas, aubergines – Madeleine moves in and out. 'Before the revolution, Moscow funerals used horses in white hoods – even the white horses! Even the black!' she says.

'What good is knowing that?' asks Choban.

'I spend hours,' she says. 'Scrolling, finding things, my archaeology. This is not the market – the market's quite indifferent, but knowing things that's obscure to all the rest – you show them, mount them, plait them like a tail. They're your rarities, your butterflies pinned on cork, they bring you forward, into the picture, in the scene: into a multitude of heads. That – it's my wisdom. Like Marley saying how he'd been a rasta "since ever since". That's a find, it makes a host of people nod and smile...'

'It seems quite trivial,' Choban says. 'Maybe I've hoist too many crates...'

'Oh,' says Madeleine, 'I'm not yet myself yet... You see – say it like that: it makes you think of Marley...'

'Marley was a person replete with his own things,' says Choban. 'He didn't need to scroll.'

'That's my point, Choban,' says Madeleine. 'You'll make it on your own. But what is new is what is called assemblage, not for you, but for the rest of us, the insignificant:... making a chain, a character, like a movie woven up from discards, frames dropped in the cutting room. You need be smart, Choban, ten times as smart as you, to make yourself from nought, like us. Real people care for you, your eccentricity, your stumbles, you hear their breath, deglutinations... The market's real – the grown-up one, I mean, not yours – those rutabagas! – but it has no eyes or ears. It's good at maths, at counting things. The rest of us – we must step out the shadows, rattle the windows, make a presence. All houses now are haunted – what a press there is! The shades, the rattlings, laughter in the grey, the growls, the mewing.'

'The codeine,' Choban says, 'we should cut down.'

'You're a genius, Choban, don't forget,' says Madeleine. 'Remember – fail big, fail quick – or else they'll eat you. Remember – there's no failure, only success. See – I'm fascinating! It isn't difficult, and no one knows, and no one cares, where I sleep, and pass my days. You're free, Choban, except the hours before the dawn and till the greenstuff has gone stale. After, you're connoisseur and impresario, prophet and tipster, conspirator, hermaphrodite...'

'I know all that,' says Choban. 'I could have been all that without the questioning, the cops.'

'Those questions purify the mind,' says Madeleine. 'You're whittled down, you lose your anecdotes, all your essentials.'

'And where are you, dear Madelaine,' he asks. 'Curled in your brain, when you're not here...?'

'Oh,' says Madeleine. 'I'm doing things you couldn't do. I have context. Those boys! The strutting! Shamans and heretics. Some smoke to cheer the continent, a pill to make it sleep ... some shooters to make an Italy, a Greece! Borgias and Calvins ... All new, all like it was!' She cackles: 'Some hope, my friend!'

'They say we must have hope,' says Choban. 'You frequent the gangs, the liberators and the hedonists – it cuts your chances down, dear Madeleine. Mine too, if you are caught...'

'You'll survive, Choban,' says Madeleine. 'Every sweet thing you say has a scaly tail – that's you. Saving yourself.'

'I'm serious, Madeleine,' says Choban. 'A shaman will take you down to hell, forget the way up again... Look at the one on the corner there, selling the tickets...'

'It's always so,' says Madeleine. 'Heaven's always the same, every time you go – they're sticked, they never close. Hell – it shifts around, they let the famished animals run up

and down the aisles, the chalice has poison and little legs
that spasm in your throat...'

'The heretics,' Choban says, 'they'll get you burnt.'

'It's true,' says Madeleine, 'they don't want converts,
only martyrs. But, Choban – I'm the sacrifice. All of us who
risk – we risk, we sacrifice – for you. We walk the edge.
We've dodgy friends and dodgy lives. You sneer at us, you
think you see our weakness – that's your privilege. But we
are the strong, the young devout and fearless ones. You're
the craven, running fearful from our smouldering bones...
"Aha, I'm too wise to end like that," you say. How true!
But – where's your wisdom, Choban? Stacking turnips in a
pyramid...?'

'Madeleine... Grown in an icicle. Chanting in a flame...'
says Choban, looking at her for the first time.

'That's only what you wouldn't want,' says Madeleine.
'It's your mantra. You disgust me. I stand naked on my
plinth, my pyre, tacked on my cross, for petty cash. Then
you frame your sketch of me, sell it for a fortune.'

'It can't be about money, Madeleine,' says Choban.
'Even too little. You never have some. No land, no sea –
that's what you explore. There'll be no map...'

'Fuck maps,' says Madeleine. 'Come with me, you're
right, there's no directions. Come after me – what do I
care?'

It's frustrating.

'Choban,' shouts Madeleine. 'You have a heritage, a
culture. That should enrich them here, where you have
ended up.'

'Gil Evans, Mulligan?' Choban asks. 'And lots of fragments – what'll they use it for? Things done as children, the sacred words – in the wind, on flags and whirligigs... The holies, with their knives...'

'Oh, read magazines,' says Madeleine. 'That's what you do. That's where the culture is.'

'Crap!' Choban says. 'Let it go. I want no more of it.'

'You lived quite poor, back where you were,' says Madeleine. 'Here, you live poor, but there's more pay.'

'I could be just normal – have no culture, or a bit of all of them,' says Choban. 'Except – I'm in a place. If I get integrated, I should bear the weight of someone else's history, the horror, all that's planned – the massacres, race hate, the empires – the running and the dead, the aspirations, the values, the sport, the executions before the dawn, before the ditch... If I don't take on their crimes – they'll watch me, I'll forever be suspected ... never be one of them. Another country – drink down all its crimes...'

'You collect bits of the good from everywhere,' says Madeleine, not convinced. 'Then again, you might get Being, get a future you'd not have back where you were; a future, not last times, nor first. Get purified, nest in one place and learn its tricks and games and incantations...'

'It would be no compensation,' Choban says. 'At best I'd be a turncoat – a freed slave exalting slavery ... the wrong colour, praising genocides... Those bits of good, they sprout from bits of bad ... they tell you, they all do, you can't pick out the best, ignore the worst. Right's twin is the wrong...'

'You should have asked the cops,' says Madeleine. 'They saw you sitting poor with Musa, seeming to talk nonsense

– here, you should be better off, a smarter culture, modern, open to what's new...'

'Look at yourself, dear Madeleine,' shouts Choban. 'Is this the Being that you want?'

'Yes, I'm a patriot,' says Madeleine. 'I am content. I do just what I want. It's turned out poorly – it could be worse, with war and pestilence.'

'Alas,' says Choban, 'here we raised a question too big for us to answer. Our lives – maybe they're too small.'

'Don't say that,' says Madeleine. 'They're said to be as big as anybody's... Maybe there's a paradox we've uncovered here. The world is one, a souk – and you're alone, set to piece together ... shards. Anyway, you must have asked the officers to have you go off somewhere, another country ... you spun the wheel...'

'All the things I want to do,' says Choban. 'Requires a document. That's why you spin the wheel. Maybe you didn't, Madeleine...'

'I didn't need to, Choban: I was born here,' she says.

'I have this dream,' says Choban. 'I have an apartment, high up, all joists and beams, holes in the floor, the walls are windows ... you could fall – the door's a trapezoid that doesn't fit into its trapezoid, there is no knob, you put a finger in the hole – and you are in, but all's a-quake, it's terrifying, but you see a landscape – oases and palms, it's peace, no one plants or harvests... It's a treetop, Madeleine, and you can't fly, your nest's just twigs laid on each other...'

'Your dream's old half a century,' says Madeleine. 'It happens so. Fold upon fold, that's how time is. There is no metaphysics, Choban, it's like a print-out, sometimes the mechanism jams and there's a sequence superimposed on many, or one's spaced out for ever. Round it goes, "a shallow stream" – there is no death, Choban, all is death, written, waiting to be reproduced. Stay clear of sex – for sure you'd fall...'

'Well, Madeleine,' says Choban. 'This is old stuff, older and older, waiting for its new turn. Bumming, slumming – it's as promising as anything, even if you feel it more, you suffer, but it's good, for it will end, you'll find the bay, the island where you'll wait, and see the cruises passing by, and wave awhile, then turn round, you're better off, there is your palmtree, hung with gifts and hampers, a fairy on the top, like you, dear Madeleine, when you were clean and held a star. And birds! What friends they are! They can't desert, this is the only tree for oceans round... Rescue – would be such a bore! There's nothing to be rescued from, except yourself, and all the goodness hanging there – bury those bottles, get plastered every day – if sailors come, they'll take you off, defile and ransom you, and have you stoke their fires...'

'Well, Choban,' says Madeleine. 'You don't stoke – you lift. The idea is the same, I guess.'

'How I love you, Madeleine...' says Choban.

'Yes,' says Madeleine. 'So – I can be off.'

*

There's nothing to be done. Since Madeleiene went, he has to think, poor Choban: there's nothing else to do. Love – he has. He needs a plan – not reading culture magazines, but economics, that way you grasp your destiny...

*

'When I was invited to the White House,' says Uwe. 'What lingers in me – the divans, chesterfields – they're never changed, from one reign to the next. They're stained, there's shells and pretzels, vomit uncleared and rings of wet. And they are grey, the carpets too, people stamp and leave black heelmarks. It's like that Russian guy, the movie about spaceships, the papers blowing... The Russians, though, they kept their office clean. I never saw a chesterfield there. They don't eat snacks, just healthy food, don't let it lie around. Ham fat is much prized.'

'You buy a lot here, Uwe,' says Choban. 'Ham, grass, corn...'

'We're all young guys,' says Uwe, boss of the tower: 'Every shape, nation, size. Mostly the others, they had modern jobs, and gave them up. The old is to be swept away, don't you agree, Choban? They've attitude. They're all used to handling keyboards. No one should do things for someone else. They'll reach the top, for sure, then just watch out! They won't give you anything, but they'll show you what they're doing. Doing like the old guys – but in the sun! Cocking their snooks. Not even half of it. A new world, with the old tower occupied. Don't look in the cellars for the core, the lovely monster – it's way up, in the attics; there's the frescoes, Matisse, music and dance. Us new world guys – we're the only lucid ones. No smoke, no pills. The rest takes things to make it bearable.'

'I know,' says Choban. 'What they take – you could make money from it, and stay clean.'

'Oh, we're clean,' says Uwe, satisfied: 'Look at the salad I've got here.'

'There will be a slogan,' says Choban.

'"Everywhere is everywhere else",' says Uwe. 'We must have an army, but it'll be a universal one. Greens, vaccines, credit, peace – those are the symbols on our flags, Choban.'

'Maybe there's a job for me,' says Choban. 'A majordomo, like – tossing the salads, distributing the oats...'

'No sarcasm, Choban,' Uwe shouts. 'That is proscribed!'

'Listen, Uwe,' Choban says. 'I'm a thinker, an artist. So, I have my afternoons free. I could come, help you guys out...'

'Which are you?' Uwe asks. 'Artist, or the other? Thinker? We live in a tower. Towers have a bad name. I like it, because you can't run out... Remember the Karl Marx Hof – built so you could mount machineguns in the bogs... We're unarmed. We don't believe in that.'

'Perhaps you should,' says Choban. 'But – that wasn't true.'

'Most things aren't,' says Uwe. 'It stops no one, though. Free sex – that's another one. We believe in plastic cash, not notes – but nothing's free. You just have debts you can't pay back. That way, you owe the rest, you pay in labour hours – only the interest, naturally, or else the whole would crumble...'

'It's ingenious,' Choban says, 'but how does sex come in?'

'Oh, you get a card,' says Uwe, pushing Choban up the corkscrewing stairs. 'There is no limit, every orifice is good – or none...'

There's windows all the way up, no frames. They stop – there's human voices, maybe from the room above. 'Feed them!' says Uwe. 'That stuff – imported grass.' Uwe screws his eyes up, into caterpillar lines, his long brown lashes, like a cow's... 'Go on!' says Uwe. 'In every cage. Everybody eats!'

'Those are beautiful', says Choban. 'Those brown rabbits... You see them like that in Moldova, white and black as well.'

'They're Belgian hares,' says Uwe.

'What's to become of them?' Choban asks.

'Decisions must be collective,' Uwe says. 'Remember the movies: "No humans were killed in the making of this spectacle..." Some humans must be, don't you think? They deserve it. Not in the movies, but before or after – what happens in between is a trick of time. Like the movies demonstrate.'

'You know, Uwe, your plan has genius,' Choban says. 'But – it lacks edge. It doesn't suck you in, though over your head it breaks... No surge, no swell, no tug, no reflux.'

'No, there's no edge,' says Uwe, laughing. 'Remember the continents – they started off as fragments in a soupy sea, and then they coalesced, like we have now, one mass, the sea disappearing – down the sinkhole, ending with a gurgle ... no more anchovies, Choban!'

'Where's the rest of you?' asks Choban.

'It's the way I look at things, Choban,' says Uwe. 'Take your time. The young guys overhead – they don't have your work experience... They're counsellors, reps, tribunes, matadors, anarchists and naughty people generally. Just now, there is an exercise – this place is safe, of course. We're all tied together by accords. It's happy times – remember, the ode...' He hums... 'Tum tum tum ti tumti – tum tum tum... Joy! Freud! But just suppose – the press gets closed, the tv's blanked, the deputies go off to jail, there's purges – schools and cops and soldiers... Are we prepared?'

'I'd guess not,' Choban says.

'The camps are opened up, they check the numbers – the wrong'uns – their numbers are already on the document... a three, a seven, woven in – you'd not suspect. You're on the system, always have been, wrong causes too don't help ... secede, amalgamate – you never know which choice is best.'

'That's always the trouble with a choice,' says Choban, out of his depth. 'You choose a country ... *on s'engage*, or else your parents choose you, should they have that fuck or not...'

'There's risk,' says Choban. 'I guess your members get the training to resist.'

'You said it, Choban,' Uwe says. 'There's always risk. You can't protect. These guys, our friends – they have no chance at all. None, zilch, I fear.'

'Why waste time, then?' Choban asks.

'Oh, it's not about resisting,' Uwe says. 'It's seeing who'll behave which way. You can't resist the crisis, Choban – it's there! Among us all!'

★

In the room above, there's people in clean jeans, staring at their screens, 'Look at me,' she says. 'I'm Melanie.'

'If that's your line,' says Choban. 'Don't hook on me. I'm a bad fish.'

'Oh,' she says. 'We're down to the last hope all round. We all have those wrong numbers, plaited in our document. Yours, Choban... Maybe a high prime – as rare as unicorns in the wood.'

'It would mean that I get off?' he asks.

'Of course not,' says Melanie. 'How would you? If you're not a refugee, you're harmless or a bad guy, sponsored, maybe, by a bank. There's nothing special in you – once you're the chosen one, that's it. You get chosen once, and then it's all dénouement.'

'The tower,' says Choban. 'It's made so's every turn opens on a different view ... it's like your screens – it twists around the world, sees everything, though it's tiny, just a rock with eyes...'

She squints: 'The spiral in the oblong? A corkscrew, Choban dear – is used to pull out corks, it's not the code of life. Look at me! Look at us – we are the new, that's all. We have no remedy. The tower, the views – Choban – it's round! All we have to stand on – is the round! Think "bottle", not a fortress, all squared off. Bottle brings you revelation, a bad mouth – knowledge and the world do not.'

'You'll all be winkled out?' asks Choban.

'You're here to bring the grass,' says Melanie. 'Feed the animals. Maybe they'll feed you.'

'It reminds me,' Choban says, 'of how you need to find a friend: That's a defence. "My Friend embraces every limb of mine, only my name remains, the rest is him..." Is Uwe your friend?'

'I hope not,' says Melanie. 'He's special. I want more from him. Think grass – that is your task. Grass – flesh: a couple, Choban. Imagine sex with me, I'll never know. We're all quite abstract here – each does what they want, but sitting at these desks. How I envy you, Choban: your comrades, all busy, dealing with the different kinds of grass and roots… Heaving, sweating, cursing… Standing on their legs…'

'I could show you how to defend yourselves…' Choban says.

'Oh no!' says Melanie. 'That means the inevitable! Military stuff? I'm dark – as you can see. I prefer a siege. Besides – I have a friend, Khalil,' and she points into the shadows.

'That's not the poetry,' says Choban. 'You've missed the point. The Friend is real but is not there. It's more than you.'

'This is security we're doing,' says Melanie. 'It's a drill. Why should they want to topple us…? Cash? Brains? Stay, Choban! After the slog – there's wine.'

'You don't make wine here,' Choban says.

'Well, here it is,' says Melanie, with a bottle, a miniature of the tower. 'We don't grow grass, we don't make flesh – sex in the building is proscribed. But flesh is here, and grass … you've brought.'

'You could be undermined,' says Choban. 'Digging. Some guys are excellent at that.'

'But why?' asks Melanie, quite merry now. 'Because we're modern? All plugged in?'

'No,' says Choban, 'because you're high. You're not tall, but you're up high. It plants the thought. Anyone could dig beneath...'

'Let's take the hares,' says Melanie, 'and run...'

This, they do.

Now, the wine's their friend, it lightens everything.

'My! They're a weight,' says Choban. 'And being kept caged here – they don't walk.'

Their arms are full of them, the ears get in their mouths, not to mention those sharp whiskers ... watch your eyes...

'We can't walk round with these,' says Melanie. 'Loose – they'd not be safe. And we've left our mates – the new wave, the guys elected, inventors of what's new – the games, the politics, riddles of existence – all that stuff... And, the tower still stands...'

'We'll find a field,' says Choban, 'without a fence, and let them run.'

They do that. The drill in the tower proceeds.

'I had a friend,' says Choban. 'She didn't need to stick around. It wasn't like the poetry says.'

'We've all had that,' says Melanie. 'It never is.'

After a while, she says, 'The rabbits. That's trouble.'

'They're used to it,' says Choban, as she climbs and climbs, to the top of the tower.

★

'I didn't find my space, Uwe,' says Choban, 'but I'm still looking for what's new.'

'That's good,' says Uwe. 'Those rabbits were my treasure – you've lost the job you didn't have for loosing them... And the tower: the tower is me. Not a bottle: it holds my spiral, body's helix. My person. Of course, it's yours, or anyone's – we're all alike. Let's be clear – the tower's not booze, not a fortress either.'

'A kind of antenna,' Choban says. 'Like on a mantis or a butterfly. Of course! People who come from where I do – there are so many histories most people don't know, don't bother with – and sides! mothers and fathers cohabiting, arriving from quite different trades and diets, feasting, fasting ... the best thing is, we, only we, know it all. Outside, they don't care – this civil, or that foreign, war ... the cities going back three thousand years have time that they belong to almost everyone, the dynasties stacked on racks like bottles ageing in the dark... So, Uwe – to each their tower, and everyone a tower, tall as tall ... those peoples intricate, the treachery, the loyalty you'd not believe...'

'Of course,' says Uwe. 'You'd all say that. You guys – from rich and ravaged lands.'

'I belong – I've belonged – to many things,' says Choban. 'I'm one of those who don't belong to countries – but I'm not in the world instead.'

'I can understand that,' Uwe says. 'I like this place – you needn't wonder where it is. There's always money coming in... I never see it – the young ones play with being chiefs, but they don't boss. I'm outside it all, though it's all me... I couldn't stand a place with hours and garbage pails, a concierge...'

'I see your people all at desks,' says Choban.

'You can't be free like you, Choban, tossed on the waves and always short of sex,' says Uwe, irritated. 'You need a culture, the passage of some history. Context, Choban – otherwise, no one can place you, you're antique. "Now this" – "not that": you have to talk like so. If you're not ready for some dirty compromise, there's nothing to renounce... Trace a straight line – how dull! You might as well drop out, drop in, and be a prof, crack codes, build atom bombs...'

'I hadn't thought of that, not any of it,' Choban says. 'I've stopped asking what comes next, or what I wouldn't want to do.'

'That often happens when a person talks to me,' says Uwe. 'What'll you do now? Leech on to Melanie? She's game ... fair game... Postcapitalism, Choban – you've heard of that, I guess? Each for themselves, away the institutions! – build the new and find your place inside... No work, just riches. That's me, I'm settled. Don't expect a hand from me.'

'Tomorrow is post-everything,' says Choban, much disturbed. 'So was today.'

'And yesterday,' Uwe chimes in. 'Don't be a lazy boy! Invent! Back where you came from – you must have brought out something you can use.'

'A terrible place,' says Choban. 'Oh! How I miss it.' And he cries. Then, 'They sell grasses on the internet – you can buy it there, Uwe.'

'It wouldn't be so fresh,' says Uwe. 'Besides, those rabbits, poor things, they'll need to take potluck, free in their field. But, Choban, you could have stayed back there, slotted in... Left those fucking hares alone! What'll we eat now, in the siege? Go home!'

'Home's gone,' says Choban. 'They've levelled it. There's thousands of us wanderers, seeking new enchantments, floating. Begging, being chivvied...' and he weeps some more.

'So,' says Uwe, embarrassed. 'You want into the tower. You've nothing left. The tower's the most. In?'

'Perhaps,' Choban snivels.

'To get in, you need success, and friends. When you're in, you get friends,' Uwe says. 'And so, success.'

'Melanie orders pants on line,' says Choban. 'That's her job.'

'One day a week,' says Uwe. 'The rest – we hack, expose, and monitor. It's puritanical, my friend. But – within, all the women are most beautiful, and salaried.'

'I've been loved,' says Choban. 'I have it still inside me. Complicity as well. Maybe that's all there is.'

'No,' Uwe says. 'There's more. Journalism. A little article – touching the earth, dodging the flying metal, eating the boiled testicle. No hotels for you. I don't mean journalism: not really. Something much better: a reporter. Scouring the sad lands.'

'You mean, go back there?' Choban asks. 'It's just a tale, a legend. There's all those scripts, twirls not on the keyboard... I can't speak or write in any one of them, no language, just picked up the everyday, the howdydo familiar.'

'That's fine,' says Uwe. 'We write it up. No metaphor, no allegory, and no quotes. Especially – no biography. You're the toad – describe the harrows. Destruction, renewal – come from the East, remember. They come with horsemen – or with wrecking balls. It's up to you – make us all shiver and enjoy...'

'If I can't write,' says Choban. 'How...?'

'You get a slate,' says Uwe. 'Like you might have had at school. There is a switch – and there I am, and you – it's a mirror that you step through when you want, but both sides reflect the same – what I want, and what you don't...'

'My friend Musa told me all about a switch. It could be that: immortality...' Choban says.

'Well, yes, but no,' says Uwe.

'And that's the way?' asks Choban. 'That's postcapitalism, the new work ... success for me ... And friends?'

'Perhaps,' says Uwe. 'We'll have to see. Don't be so academic. Think lotus: open up!'

*

'Farewell, then, Choban,' Melanie says. 'Uwe's got rid of you – that was an easy thrust. What's your fate? Journalist? Reporting? So much better. We in the tower, already we know everything: the world, entire. You'll be a target. Who's interested, anyway, in what you see? Do they talk Kosova, Azawad, round here? The rich, the poor, the flooded, and the thirsty – all far away... Good for them, unless they fight us back...'

'Oh,' Choban says, 'I'm full of nuances. Uwe must think well of me, if he's sent me out to die. The cause is noble, and demanding... Biblical, indeed.'

'If you're content...' says Melanie. 'It's good. My job... its advantage is, there's not a scent of death. We're paid sums so immense, no bank could pay us, not a fraction. We'll give it all away... We're rich, we sleep on chairs, eat stuff in cellophane... No sex – and best of all, no death. Why are you here, Choban? All that goes on here – stays in the tower. The values, the world, the future – all upstairs. Just like it used to be, when there were kings.'

'I read all that somewhere,' says Choban. 'But, I'll see the thing direct.'

'Not as direct as us,' says Melanie. 'Kosova – those lovely forests, like they used to be. The desert: before the wars, the droughts – so full of folk, the songs, the big idea, the freedom ... the Tuaregs' good times...'

'It seems your pictures – stick in the past,' says Choban.

'People like it so,' says Melanie. 'That's obvious. But – tell me, Choban – what do I look like? We have no room for mirrors here. What's my face, my body, like?'

'Oh, it's quite good,' says Choban. 'The stare: you mustn't stare.'

She isn't pleased. 'Why did you come, Choban? Not cash! Maybe you think – "control my destiny".'

'They used to say, "God has the power", but doesn't use it, from respect, or curiosity. Now, saving the world – it's complicated for the powerful guys,' Choban says. 'Maybe that task obstructs what they'd set out to do. It's not what you're supposed to bring, salvation. No one so far has ever managed it...'

'You wander, Choban, and so of course, there's bad and better all the way,' she says.

'Oh, I expect it's love that drives,' says Choban. 'That's what they say. And, being my free and potent self...'

'Love drives you, but it doesn't perch, it doesn't fly, not up to the bushy top,' she says. 'Besides – I thought for people, people like you, it means something different. On the steppe, maybe, in the desert, but once you got civilised – it was all formal and kids. Maybe some quatrains...'

'I'm full of love,' says Choban. 'Melanie – would there be room to add you on, or am I replete with love for Madeleine? I'll never see her more, that is for sure. Maybe it's the same with you, if I am in the forefront, get struck down...Where does love go, how does it die, when I am gone? Is it mere metaphysics, piling a love on love, quantity on quantity... quality on quality...? Loving not two women, any two, just any persons, say, a man, woman, and a cat: love's always you, in you, not them. Does love stay, when all its objects die? You're always loving absences: a person, scent, a sentence – just, not there. Not present, ever. Nowhere, loving no one, you're somewhere living on a "nothing", a no-man's land, where that's the name of everything: Nothing... That's love. A void.'

'We don't touch that, Choban,' says Melanie, holding him against her breasts: 'Love's like that, the true sort – it all depends who you send the postcards to, the one who gets your ashes... And is that love? Dust handed on? I hadn't thought that deep...'

'It's like junket,' Choban says. 'Love slips down – but it's a special kind, not digested...'

'Are you sure?' asks Melanie. 'Some people, maybe, assimilate, but there's others, down it goes, it's more like stale pie, or crumbled brick ... and in the past – it was a nourishment, but came out later on your skin, like protein tumours, waxy scales...'

'Where Uwe's sending me,' says Choban. 'A wandering Hittite, once again! The people must be hard: sad, and angry. All emotions, like a Macedonia, people living hugger-mugger – bats in a cave... you can't say those sentiments are not digested.'

'For me, it's a blind angle,' Melanie says. 'I can't describe them, these emotions. The book says I don't love you, so I'll go along with that. But then – the book says love's an obligation, even if there's nothing there.'

'Uwe's not sending me to any place,' says Choban. 'Nothing specific – just where I hear cries. He is the greedy king. So, I can wander on, or settle in. There must be danger... That's not an emotion, I suppose, although you feel it... Even if there's none. It might be true for lots – choice, meaning – all arrived at on the wing, fleeting, though, dandelion clocks, what you think, what you feel, all a tingle in the head...'

'To be frank, Choban,' says Melanie. 'Don't put things like that in any stuff you send us in the tower. It won't go down, not like junket, not like pie. Forget it, forget metaphor and simile.'

'Then, yes, you're right – there is forgetting things, there's loss...' says Choban.

'Most of everything is lost,' says Melanie. 'Though, you can dig it up.'

'No,' says Choban. 'What I want, you can't. To build a stupa on the plain – immense; wherever you are, so it always looks the same far off. Perspective, not faith. To ride with silent horsemen ... thousands...'

'You see, Choban, when you tell me what you are – I don't feel anything,' says Melanie.

'Perhaps you will when I'm not there,' says Choban.

'Perhaps, yes,' says Melanie. 'You're strange, Choban.'

'The past – out it comes,' says Choban. 'Don't ask a child "what do you want to be?" They'll have to memorise the possibilities, the awful ones.'

'Khalil is tranquil, he respects...' says Melanie. 'Then there's my special, Uwe.'

'What I might want to be – it may never come about,' says Choban. 'It's not a threat, and I'm not cruel. Ambitious, though. My friend Musa – he was the gifted one.' He sighs, it's memory, unpurged... 'We're little buns – they bake us, we end up on the asphalt, for the pigeons. What I might want to be, I can't.'

'That's always worse,' says Melanie. 'Knowing and wanting. There's mortality, sharpening its sword.'

*

The tower – it's not secure. They take the shape, and build it upside down, a bunker, bottom what was top. Inside, they're all still looking for that switch – the one that Musa couldn't seek... Melanie the keenest searcher of them all.

'It doesn't matter,' Choban thinks. 'Who's here, immortal or just transiting – it makes no difference. Keep it like it is, suppose the void waits for everything. It's just the same, eternity and dust – you can't tell anything by looking at the face. Forget all that, the speculation, and accept the ends, the question unanswered, cut off before its mark is reached.'

*

He's blown away. The wind? – why not? It blows in everywhere. Living with the families besieged, their roofs of concrete, roofs of silk, of felt, of grass. Roofs on a screen, in someone's sights, dark clouds. He's worming into everywhere: he's paid for it. Neither he, nor they – they can't do anything.

He's there, beside them, but can't speak, you don't see him in the mirror... Choban could talk about the humanity, tough unresolving lives, soft promises – but he won't. That's fiction. He's a stylist, he can't use metaphor. His ethic binds him. Everybody knows how hard things are – how you need to be a hero, every day.

If he addresses something to the tower, Uwe doesn't look at it.

If you're a reporter, you don't get anywhere with being it: except you go on, to another place.

4

THE ANSWER

'IT WAS ON THE BORDER of the County of Tain. It was magnificent – like two centuries ago – a palette of trees, as they say, every green, orange and brown, donkeys abounding, rain squalls and tender sun, hills with tiny castles and big stables up the sides. I'd not thought of the Republic like this – that rural stretch, a passage for arms and fugitives... Coming from the other side, the Monarchy, you carry the picture that the Republic's far ahead, cemented, not rustic, but rusting. Over in the kingdom, there's the royals – I've never seen them – they're reclusive, ga-ga, they say, syphilis from rituals repetitive, exhaustive, entrails inspected, guns dragged or shouldered, salutes by numbers.'

Pascal's vision. He's triumphant. Peace!

'If it's insults or provocation – that's not our game, you know,' says the know all, Alfonse. 'Royals are an asset. Alfonse – kings of Portugal – then came Brazil – tropical songs, the birds, the whistling. Marvellous! It's me, if you doubted it – beneath the skin, of course. Now – are we reduced? I doubt it. Innovation and entertainment's what we do. They're part of it, those old queens and kings.

They're up there so we can sneak things in, wait for unexpected consequences, the awful ones, and give them gloss. The future's green, Pascal, and then it's brown and on the ground, then in those black bags. Derision? – forget it, little man. I'll bring you down! You know I'm capable of that ... I'll wipe you out.'

And he will.

Four sit round the table – those two, and Pearl, drawing a caricature of Alfonse – is it what you know or only what you see? A round head, a beak, sallow, black-peppered skin, she even puts the colours in. She's from some part of China, maybe from its spread, diaspora, a past disclaimed.

And mostly silent – Ashok.

'A video game for soldiers. Set in no place... To pass their last hours. Not hard: frustrating, a dream. Full of platforms you can't reach,' she says.

'Not no place,' says Alfonse. 'Every place, and every time. Suited for Jihadis too – they love the games, apocalypse – they're passionate, no lies, no cheating... Just the programme.'

'There's a contradiction,' Pascal says. 'They have children, yet their end is gravid in those clouds... I castrate my cats, because I know that life is hard. Placing the little ones – you know how it concludes.'

These four – collect ideas. Innovation, entertainment: let them out the vase, they'll boom around the system. Acocalypse, but no one will suspect. At first, it's play. Those four – each knows a quarter of the tale. You need a narrator – there! – maybe she's up there, in the corner, just one electric eye. You wouldn't want to see it reeling out from her, reality ... watching nothing happening all night –

that was a Sixties thing, when everyone had time to waste...
You need film editors, then cameras placed all over – the
elevator, washrooms: even, if the four go out that room –
outside.

They have no cash. They take your plan, go somewhere
else – pester a fund – and make the spiel to get the paper
backing for a launch...

'Mostly,' Ashok says, 'every game is suitable for soldiers.
The training, falling in the tutti frutti...'

'Not so,' says Pearl. 'Some games are like Tain County.
Trees – and people trying to escape.'

'That was Pascal,' says Alfonse. 'Romancing. Trees,
steep hills like those above Savona. He dreamed it. He
doesn't have a bicycle.'

'Oh,' Pearl says, 'You rent them. That's the latest thing.'

★

I spoke to Pearl, long past. 'Inflatable?' she laughs. 'Child's
overcoats? Because you once fell in the river, couldn't
swim? How many would that save? Besides, they're not
worn any more... Green, horn buttons? What a laugh. A
crap idea – expensive too. Away with it, your coddling
humanism!'

And so, we knew about each other, all there was to know,
and we never spoke again.

The unknown shades, saved, carried downstream to the
rocks: dark bladders, waving... Those drowning kids – I
wasn't all that interested. It was me, the waifish child, the
mystery of what I'd been – that, I wanted to preserve. To

rescue. Discover and explore, the misty land, gone, gone, for good and bad. The others? They should watch out.

'And you didn't drown,' said Pearl. 'If you had, things would be different, less tortuous, less perverse. Less of what you think's the norm.'

*

'Toys,' says Ashok. 'They skitter off, and you fall in the stream. Perfect! It's the quest – no price, no sacrifice, for you or all the rest, suffices, as they slip away: the yacht you'll never own, the submarine you'll serve in – will it sink? It can't, already it is sunk, and you spend your years wondering why you haven't drowned... The football, on the billows – "pass, pass!" "shoot, shoot" – and so you try to pass. Pass by, pass on. No hope. Religion – what your grannie told you – you can't pass that!

'So – it's "shoot!" with the gun you coveted...! We'll shrink it down... a little gallery, pocket size your toy, a corridor that holds the infant and the senile, the whole life-world... Then – when you're aggravated, it's become a shooting gallery! Those pictures! Faces, at their end, understanding everything. And we're in there: we devise the game, and then the novelty. A country without its novelties is dead; cities of the deformed, of the nets... like Moscow when there weren't bananas – how the rest mocked! Now there's kakis – too dear for you, but no one laughs...'

He's silent. The rest laugh.

Alfonse says, 'I can't stand kakis. We all wish we could start again, Ashok, and get it right. It's good we can't, and stumble on, the royals ride past, the coachmen with their gristly heads, the king all blabbery, the queen sagged down... Don't laugh! Fifty metres distance – your own face is a blob, your head a lucifer – scratch it ... pouf! And up you go in flame...!'

'We must put ourselves in a frame, Alfonse,' Pascal says, 'or – we should make a frame that fits us all. Think of Piranesi. Think of four buildings, each with a purpose, making one structure...'

'A zoo, a morgue, a prison, and a game,' says Pearl. 'The game: can hold those three, and it's the fourth building, but it holds a multiplicity of other buildings, some on paper, some in blue or sketch or in a petrie dish...'

'I don't see it, Pearl,' Alfonse says. 'Typically, it's not thought through.. Are these structures superimposed? Do they intersect? Do you see them, are you confined in them, an animal in its cage – or just you labour in them? We know that modern work – is quite impossible. No slave was ever bound to such frustration, such limits without hope of manumission. Where is all that, Pearl? We control those purposes – you call them four, like us – we four. Like horsemen. We have broken free from work, that's why we have control – but our "everything", of which we make our ten percent, is just a sample of what is. Are we in the picture – or is the picture us? We rule the roost – but mustn't crow. We can't.'

'You mustn't write things down,' says Pearl. 'A person written – they are small, contested. Their arms and legs are just a brushstroke. Like a cross upon two struts. A yoke upon a fork. You write, you draw – you, an other – they're a miniature, a copy, a multiple.'

'Oh no!' shouts Alfonse. 'Now, Pearl, you're like Pascal, Tain County. The trees, the green, the eye belonging to no person, cycling on the unmade road... If you don't make it up yourself, there is no story, and no sentimental cyclist. No conventional signs! Make it all new! Decide, control!'

'I didn't mean that, Alfonse,' Pearl objects. 'Not once. I'm pleased that I'm a boss. Not everywoman.'

'We don't boss anything,' says Ashok. 'We facilitate. We stick bits of nothing with someone else's glue, and make reality.'

'That must count for something,' Alfonse says.

In the County of Tain, that Pascal says he saw – might have seen – no one worked. That makes it a dream, and makes us doubt he didn't see a thing, just thought he did.

'Work is life,' Alfonse says. 'Without it, we all die. Remember those vast peasant armies, the herders – on their ponies, the Vikings taking slaves each summer – all work; all dull, all dangerous. All life.'

'Dance. That is the game,' says Ashok.

'Not if it doesn't rain,' says Alfonse. 'And – hey guys! I don't enjoy always being right. Sounding right.'

'Maybe you should take a rest, Alfonse,' Pascal says. 'Being right – it takes its toll.'

'Fight, man!' shouts Alfonse. 'Don't think of bringing in someone else – four is just right. Fight to preserve yourself – not to dilute. Maybe you'll win our duel – I doubt it. Don't be so cowardly...'

'He's quite right,' says Pearl. 'The ten percent we take – is not a lot. But ten percent of everything – it's more than any other four can have. No one to work for us, nothing written down.'

'There are no other four like us,' says Alfonse, irritated. 'Fewer? It could work: there's Nero and his paints, or Heliogabalus and his prayers and sacrifice. They went solo! No, four's correct. Pascal, for opium – life style, melody – the folk. To each their culture, listen to all the rest on stream. It soothes, guys go into battle with their music plugged into their ears. It's dancing time!

'Pearl with finance – the making things and paying off, the demolitions – change. Energy – and lassitude. The chairs we sit on while we await our daily bread – our welfare.

'Ashok – we needed paradox – war and security, that's yours. Upgrading weapons, digging holes to hide them in. And I do all the rest. There's nothing else. No "five", Pascal; no stranger at our feast: no "something else", no "maybe there is more", a residue, a future or a "next". Before we came, the men were slugs – viscid and slow, subsistence freaks. We gave them shells. Now they can carry luxury, a universe, upon their backs. Be mindful of the thrushes, that is all – we can't give eternal life, but we can make death a delicate surprise – a squawk, tap tap your shell upon a stone – it's done! You're down a throat! The song goes on. No regrets – the song, it wasn't yours, not yours to make it up. After all, you're just a snail. Maybe up there – down there, if you live down south – one day soon, they'll make an empire in the stars. For sure, they'll find more snails out there. Anyway, Pearl's taking care of everything. She buys the rocket, and the bottle you must launch it from... Snails everywhere, my friends: and just like me! My comrades: not my image, but distant relatives, the buzzing mix of crawling round you see outside...'

'That sounds quite *facho*,' Pascal says. 'We only deal with ten per cent ... not with how much people's worth...'

'But that's the most,' Alfonse says. 'Ten per cent's omnipotence. Just one per cent, that pile of notes won't fit into your shoes. Two per cent – the cellar's full of gold. Ten per cent – is far too much to stash. It's quality, my friends: it's Spirit. Being. We're the happy ones, the ones who spin and weave the pattern in...'

'This room,' says Pearl. 'If one were that sort, one could make love in it – use those grey armchairs – when we're here, everybody sits straight up on steel and leatherette.'

'Someone else rents this space, almost always,' Alfonse says. 'You'd need to choose your time.'

'Oh, short,' says Pearl. 'My time's like that – although it's meaningless to speak of time. While you are talking – there it goes! Short and sweet? That's your span, your time. You hope! But – real time's a vodka, long and prickly. It doesn't fit, you and what's real; going on without you! But something sweet? Mmmm. Out of time! Can sex be sweet?'

'Think of a stick of rock,' says Alfonse, touching her: 'With "Happy memories" inside, along its length.'

'Oh, memories,' says Pearl, scuttering away. 'To me, memories are quite like time: not happy, and not sad. Best clothes, hung up and silent in the dark.'

'It's like the communists,' Alfonse says. 'When I was one, they were quite saints. And common sense prevailed in discourse – only after, I saw that if you mean a thing, you don't roll over when there's storm and lightning. You use your pitchfork, and your lawyers. Time goes usually by, that's fine. But fill it up with bangs and famine, and it's full of rage.'

'Euphoria got dull,' says Pearl. 'Changing everything, the politics. Then we found everything had all been different from what we ourselves had seen, close to. And nothing like what got written down. When it was history, it became quite unrecognisable. That's quite a paradox. It's like computers. I have a psychotic interlude when I go inside – it's a flat world, where there is every thing, there's just one dimension, flat, and yet – in you fall. No splash. You don't seem to drown. There is a depth that doesn't fit the universe... It's unique, a cave without a depth – just figures painted dancing on the wall. A man – you make him with a cross, a fork. They say that space is mostly plasma – like a tv screen – but if you're buying underwear on line, it seems there's rules and interdictions you have not been taught, they seem authoritative. No one is listening. There's commands, though. You feel like screaming, but of course, you're in a corridor with cells along – if they hear, they can't get out to help...'

'Who?' asks Pascal. 'Who is in those cells?'

'Spies,' says Pearl. 'And shopkeepers.'

'You shouldn't enter there,' says Ashok. 'It's unpredictable, what trace you leave... Writing, now, without a contract, no one even knows you're literate. But tap-tap on the keys...! You sculpt! Don't trust it, Pearl.'

'Do you have a place where you often stay, Pearl? To sleep, and so on?' Pascal asks.

'Why does that excite you, Pascal?' Pearl asks. 'As it happens – I mostly move around. They say the basis of it all, our life stacked up but edging on, must be the incest tabu. On the march, you've better chances to avoid it. No structuring, and so you don't risk anathema. Besides, a pile of good memories of different spots keeps us purring in old age. The more you've been in different places, better's the chance you'll have those memory snaps you can browse through. So – you escape the main tabu: incest. Everyone's a stranger.'

'Quite right,' says Ashok. 'Structures abound. They're meaningless. Every snowflake has one, till it melts, then there's another. It's all design. It pleases. There's no meaning. It's like touching regular the objects on your desk, scratching your face... You can get sucked in – to family, to being old or young, this or that gender – a taste in singers, colours, food that's cooked this way or that – order, sequence, architecture, classes – it is all a tic.'

'You know,' says Pascal. 'People think we don't exist. Or if we do, it's for the cash.'

'It's better so,' says Pearl. 'That's why we do what we do.'

'How we do it too... People are slices of other people,' Ashok says. 'Almost everyone exists. There's only so many ways you can assemble them.'

'That's the real you're talking about,' Pascal says. 'There is the real, then there's how we wish it were. Simpler, or kinder. Longer lasting, letting us go free.'

'No,' Ashok says. 'That's not it at all. That kind of existence is hypothetical. The real is not, not at all. People know – it shimmies up and down, the real, yours is not mine. And – it's not good. No one would make it like it is, or want to live in it. Here we are: in that, we have no choice.

It's angels and devils, and everyone in between. Of course – between those two, there is no "in between". You're one or other. I don't think we four make it all much better, or much worse. Here we are.'

'Of course, Ashok, I trust you,' Alfonse says. 'It's my selfless thought, though, that – Pascal's our weakest link.'

'There must be one,' says Ashok. 'And it's the strongest link that breaks the chain.'

'When you're a drinker,' Alfonse says. 'All your friends are drinkers too. Advice? – it's useless!'

Pearl says, 'Drinking's vital to his task. And painted or excised – Pascal's in charge of skin. They're vital for us humans: the wine. The sex. The song.'

'If you're pissed, those all end up the same,' says Ashok.

'That's it,' says Alfonse. 'It's innovation, novelty. Pascal, the Dionysius of life! It rocks the ship. I thought you'd have a gadget that would keep him quiet, Ashok. His special petard.'

'Skins are nearly silent,' Ashok says. 'Even the snake's. You have to leave your old clothes on the floor, flaunt in the new. It's the song, Alfonse, that's got to you: if it's too loud for you … just turn it down!'

★

'Ashok's dim,' Alfonse says to Pearl. 'He doesn't understand. Pascal's mind is on his bike – soundless, who knows where he trundles?'

'We're new,' says Pearl. 'We have no nationality, no nation ancient, forced, idealised. And we're not ephemeral, elected. We have no Sykes, no Picot, no promise made, none broken. Beholden to no one – we shan't fail, because we have no hope, no project, no victory of the good's in sight, no massacre of the bad...'

'Exactly so,' says Alfonse. 'There's something missing. It doesn't sound so new. You make us sound like shits, like bankers, like shepherd kings... Come down out the sun.'

'My father was a black man,' says Pearl. 'My foster. The best man who ever lived. Scum who says otherwise...'

'Where you getting to, Pearl?' asks Alfonse, not impressed.

'The Brits were worst,' says Pearl. 'They were around for wider, longer. Rule and divide. Those pale ghosts!'

'That's gone,' says Alfonse. 'I vote against the past. Ashok is right – we just facilitate. We're fucking bankers. We should raise our eyes...'

'Pascal chooses our tomorrows. He bets on what will stick, and throws the rest away,' says Pearl. 'That's how we live tomorrow – movies and groups, and gadgets too. There's carnage – oversupply. All that music wasted, guys trudging round with gazoos, the monks, imams, those sermons about humankind and leaping up – piled high and stinking in the back room, never heard or seen again...'

'Monks don't do sermons,' Pascal says. 'They do thin lives, and leave no bones.'

'We're madams of the Rising Sun,' shouts Alfonse. 'Running rich whores. The clients have the hard luck – all clapped out...'

'Like the royals,' says Pascal. 'You didn't like my take on that...'

'Away with clients!' Alfonse says. 'Rich or not. They can't help it – the lust, the pulse, spending what may not return. The everlasting tickle. No one can help themselves. At least we don't pretend, we're not elected, won't step down...'

'What then?' asks Ashok. 'What we do now, we do well. And no one sees us, no one sees the curtain move, the hidden hand that saws the ladies and the gents in half...'

*

They're exhausted. 'What we should do,' says Ashok. 'Is see what clings. Each makes a tour – what peoples, places, things laid in the sun and in the nursery trunk, all laid out that's what we want to be, to see – then we shall know what binds us four, what's the next step.'

'Trees?' asks Alfonse. 'Leaves?' – disparaging.

'Oh, more than that, let's say,' says Ashok, and he laughs. 'Less, maybe. Each decides – I know, for myself... Death – a death without a vowel. Smrt. It should be "*smert*"', but they were right, without a vowel – it is more satisfying. Alpha and omega, those are the vowels that count, the rest is lubricant. Without a vowel, death's what we can all pronounce and recognise – the only word that's so... I'll find a rock, sit with my flute – the holes are vowels: mine, for me. It's not my tibia, that flute – it's maybe someone else's, a casual find... To do our music, we are the voyagers, the virtuosi, playing up the invisible stairways, down to the rumbling cellars... Wind, my friends. That's all it is, wind, not death, wind blows it all away, and drags you in to its white bulk while it goes on and onward – that's where the music sprawls and sings, it's not that huckster stuff, gunpowder and its bangs... Hear it, it's melody, the force of breath... Calm! The passage of the air – you can get used to it, it does the breathing for you... Those munitions – they inhale, regenerate: they're a spat, a twirl of dust, then all is flat, you start again, the creatures crawl up out the mud, they grow a crest, then stumps, and then philosophy. They turn their muzzles to the breeze – and here it comes! The new, scirocco, then the storm, and everything lies down before it, and all is mud again...'

'Yes, Ashok,' Alfonse says. 'But where's the project, the project we could use, all four of us? You must trade something suitable. It all explodes, expends, and reappears. Is there nothing more than that?'

'Security?' says Ashok. 'Making it all safe, defused. Where's the project there? Those arms we sell, that bring security, and don't.'

'Well, Pearl,' says Alfonse. 'Where'll you take us?'

'From down here, they look like buttocks, you go lyrical, putting them in other words,' says Pearl. 'Buttocks. Clouds. But when you go up there – they are different. The athletes have these litle wings – you wear, you jump, you fly... And when you're up – you see close to, the buttocks – they are faces, seams of steam, and dust of coal and gold. Wealth ephemeral – you hug them – and they leave you wet and cold...'

'You come down – again, they're buttocks,' Alfonse says.

'You stay aloft – they're cheeks and breasts – you are the hawk, they transmogrify, but you are hunting, always on the move,' says Pearl. 'Afloat.'

'How dull,' says Alfonse. 'Fatalism, the ephemeral, all in the sky, wind and cloud. So, what are you, Pascal? In the mulch? Some heathrug animal, eyes down, looking for its grubs?'

'I'm disappointed too,' Pascal says. 'Ashok I understand – his fireworks going up in aahs, the glistering clusters lying round and feared, so tempting, so "don't touch"... But – Pearl! The banks, the treasure – my dear, the capital! How could you think to drift, wearing those psychedelic colours! Jumping off a height! Spreading your cape like Mercury... Where's the drama, Pearl? Clouds! You should have brought us capital, the history, the works!'

'It *is* Capital, you idiot,' says Pearl. 'Those clouds, the Mercury, my leap, parabola, buttocks – the rain, the drizzle...'

'There's no story, Pearl,' says Alfonse. 'It's just drift. You, jumping, flapping little wings. Nature: just like leaves and trees.'

'Oh,' says Pearl. 'Clouds go on, when all the leaves are down, and trunks are burnt.'

'For sure,' Alfonse says. 'Pascal will tell us that without the trees, there are no clouds...'

'Oh no,' says Pascal. 'That was only my epiphany. I deal with the residue. The style, the culture – the creation. It all comes from the street...'

'Don't tell us, Pascal,' Alfonse says. 'It all grows by itself, it's all a sport of nature... The strength comes from the street, the commonplace, the lurid, the peppery...'

'No, no,' says Pascal. 'What you call culture – it's made by losers. Like the trees: – those are losers too...the tumbling leaves, the cutting into planks and two-by-twos...'

'That's quite banal,' says Pearl. 'The street's alive because of housing – you can't live in it, so out you go ... into the world of deaf composers, crazy painters, clumsy jugglers... That's the street – a run of rickety creations, unfinished manuscripts, unreadable ... narcissistic lyrics, paintings where the paint's gone rigid in the tube – a thousandth part gets taken up and sold, scraped off the asphalt, spooned off the earth – and that's what we dance to, that's what pedals in our brain, that gerbil's wheel, the villanelle, the leitmotif, the crumpled flower stuck in a lumpish vase...'

'Yes,' says Pascal, uncomfortable. 'Some find it quite miraculous, that from the mud there springs...'

'...a raging virus. I understand,' Alfonse says. 'That all this residue – the sound, the song, this human plenitude – this run of eels, this hatch of may – that all this is abundance quite involuntary. Spawn. A gelatine of mouths and tiny hips, all wiggling, all searching for a scrap of cast-off food, some krill, some plankton – street food in a greasy screw – just enough to keep the creature up and running till it fornicates and dies, and off existence goes again... It's fascinating, Pascal. So, that's our female side? Don't spread it round, Pascal, that that is what they call *ewige Kunst...* It seems there's not a project here. Pascal's culture – it's just life automatic, pullulating. No need for banks or capital. No Pearl. No oyster. A struggle for some food needs no artillery. No Ashok. We go on as we are, it seems. It's disappointing. But – we are a step head, a level higher then the instinct. As for me – I could say my role, my destiny is: always on the right, the good, side. Keeping us from slipping back into the hunger, the subsistence, the rite of sex and pasta, ages of anxiety and strife. So! *Davai, davai! Allons, enfants...!* That is it... Alas!'

'What we do,' says Ashok. 'We do supremely well.'

'We'd do it just as well without Pascal,' says Alfonse. 'The culture comes quite automatically – a baby's cry, a parrot's squawk... The dream, Tain County!'

★

They can surely do without Pascal. Lifestyle, the muzak and the murals – takes care of itself. Most you don't ever see. Besides, this searching for a project – that's gone by, obsolete: like when monks asked for a Deposition, something chic in terra cotta... And it's better so.

'Have no fear,' says Alfonse. 'You two, Pearl, Ashok, are safe. And tell me Pearl – do you have someone check your wings before you leap?'

'Of course!' she says. 'That's the essential part. The rest is nature.'

'If it's so perilous, my dear,' says Alfonse. 'Why d'you do it?'

'It's to show my confidence,' says Pearl...

'In something you can't trust,' Alfonse finishes. 'And you, Ashok – I hope you don't test the stuff you deal?'

'Oh no,' says Ashok. 'There's a fuss for each mistake.'

'Well,' Alfonse says. 'We all know what is good and right. In the end, we have to trust our judgement. Others too will judge, of course – there's nothing you can do about that. Life's a web, a net. A tangle that bears us to the frying-pan. We're alert to all such complications – and we even found the answer. How to make your mark: even the modest splash that no one sees or hears ... it's you, you, going down...'

The other two, Ashok and Pearl, are quiet. Alfonse says:

'It's clear. You need not four, not four abreast, but three's enough.'

ABOUT THE AUTHOR

John Fraser has lived in Rome since 1980. Previously, he worked in England and Canada.

www.ingramcontent.com/pod-product-compliance
Lightning Source LLC
Chambersburg PA
CBHW030313180626
46810CB00003B/1064